MW01533421

CONTENTS

UNLOCKING THE MAGIC – BOOK 1: A SORCERER'S BRAVE AWAKENING

CHAPTER 1

The battlefield reeked of coppery blood and charred flesh, the acrid stench mingling with the sulfurous tang of unnatural energy. Every gust of wind carried the moans of the dying and the wet squelch of torn bodies crushed underfoot. The twisted beasts pouring forth from the rift were a nightmare made flesh—misshapen horrors that should not exist in any sane reality. Their grotesque forms shifted in the sickly green glow of the rift, each abomination a patchwork of misplaced limbs, gnashing fangs, and lidless, staring eyes.

The rift itself was a wound in the fabric of existence, a jagged, pulsing gash rimmed with an undulating, fleshy edge that oozed black ichor. It breathed like a living thing, exhaling waves of corrupt energy that warped the ground beneath it. Grass and flowers wilted into sludge, while stones cracked and split, spewing faint wisps of steam. Zarathyn stood in the eye of this hellstorm, his figure outlined in the pale, eerie light spilling from the abyss.

Raw magic crackled around him, the currents

so dense that the air itself shimmered, heavy with its charge. His once-pristine robes hung in tatters, streaked with blood and soot. Burn marks marred the exposed flesh of his arms, but the pain had long since dulled under the weight of his determination. The crystal atop his staff pulsed faintly, its light dimming as the effort of the battle began to take its toll.

His deep, resonant voice cut through the chaos, the cadence of his ancient incantation rising and falling like a storm's tide. As he spoke, the sky above mirrored his power, splitting open to reveal arcs of violet lightning. Each bolt slammed into the earth with a deafening crack, leaving scorched craters and obliterating the nearest monstrosities. The beasts nearest to him, too malformed to scream properly, burst apart in sprays of ichor and bone, their putrid remains sizzling where they landed.

But the surge of relief was fleeting. For every abomination he obliterated, two more crawled forth, clambering over the corpses of their kin with mindless hunger. They came on all fours, their claws scraping deep furrows into the blood-soaked ground. Some moved on six limbs, their bodies serpentine and coiled, while others lumbered on massive legs that ended in hoof-like stumps. Their distorted faces were a cruel parody of life—jaws unhinging to reveal multiple rows of jagged teeth, tongues slithering like worms.

A pack of smaller creatures surged ahead,

their spindly limbs propelling them forward with unnatural speed. They snapped their needle-thin jaws as they closed the distance, their beady eyes fixed on the archmage. Zarathyn swept his staff in a wide arc, and a ripple of kinetic force shot forth, hurling the creatures back. Their bodies collided with the earth, shattering like brittle clay, but still, the tide surged.

One beast, larger than the rest, shoved its way through the chaos. Its grotesque frame was hunched and swollen, its misshapen limbs bulging with unnatural muscle. Eyes—too many eyes—glowed a faint green as it fixed its gaze on Zarathyn. It let out a deep, guttural roar that rattled the bones of the fallen knights, its massive claws carving deep furrows into the dirt as it charged.

Zarathyn thrust his staff forward, the crystal at its tip blazing brighter than before. A spear of pure energy erupted from the weapon, slamming into the beast's chest. The impact tore a gaping hole through its torso, spraying blackened gore across the battlefield. The creature staggered, its malformed limbs flailing wildly before it collapsed in a heap of twitching flesh.

And still, they came.

Zarathyn's breath hitched, his chest heaving under the strain. The tide was unrelenting, the creatures inexhaustible. The rift pulsed again, vomiting more of the horrors into the world, their grotesque bodies lit in its unholy glow. He could feel his reserves dwindling, the raw power that had once made him unstoppable now slipping through his grasp.

Behind him lay the remnants of the king's finest warriors. Their armor, once gleaming, was torn open like paper. The knights had fought valiantly, their blades biting deep into monstrous flesh, but it wasn't enough. Even now, their blood painted the ground in a macabre tapestry of valor and futility.

Zarathyn raised his staff, the silver crystal atop it glowing brighter than the rift itself. With a sweep of his arm, he summoned a wall of fire that roared to life, splitting the battlefield in two. The creatures screeched as the flames consumed them, their bodies writhing in agony before collapsing into smoldering heaps.

Still, the rift churned. The fire slowed the horde but did not stop it. Zarathyn's breath came in ragged gasps, his strength waning. His mind raced through spells and strategies, searching for something, anything, to turn the tide.

Then he saw it—a knight, barely clinging to life, crawling toward him. The man's helmet was gone, revealing a face marred with claw marks. His lips moved, but no sound came. With trembling hands, he offered up his sword.

Zarathyn took it without a word. It was a simple blade, its edge dull from overuse, but it would have to do. He plunged it into the ground, channeling what little magic the weapon could hold. The earth trembled. Pillars of stone erupted around the rift, their surfaces glowing with runes of containment.

The creatures hesitated for the first time, their grotesque heads turning toward the rift as if sensing the shift in the battle. Zarathyn gritted his teeth and poured more power into the spell. The pillars began to hum, the runes spinning faster.

But the effort was draining him. His vision blurred, and his legs threatened to give out. He stumbled, catching himself on the sword. The rift pulsed violently, resisting his attempt to contain it.

"No," Zarathyn growled. His voice, though hoarse, carried the weight of unyielding will. "You will not have this world."

The beasts surged again, sensing his weakness. Zarathyn met them with raw fury, summoning a storm of ice shards that ripped through their ranks. The shards struck true, piercing skulls and severing limbs. The ground was slick with black blood, the air thick with the stench of decay.

Still, they came.

A clawed monstrosity leapt at him, its jaws wide enough to swallow his head. Zarathyn swung the staff like a cudgel, cracking its skull with a sickening crunch. Another lunged from the side, its talons aiming for his throat. He thrust a hand forward, unleashing a burst of kinetic force that sent the creature hurtling into the rift.

The edges of his vision darkened. His hands

trembled as he lifted the staff again, the crystal now dim. He could feel the rift pulling at him, demanding more than he had left to give.

And then it came to him—the spell. A forbidden incantation, locked away in the deepest recesses of his mind. It would cost him everything, but it would end this.

Zarathyn planted his feet and raised the staff high. The air around him shimmered with heat as he began the chant. The words tore at his throat, their power too vast for mortal speech. The staff's crystal flared, casting the battlefield in blinding light.

The creatures howled in unison, their bodies convulsing as the spell took hold. The rift began to collapse, its green light flickering and fading. The pull of its energy grew stronger, drawing the beasts back into its maw.

The tide of horrors continued, unrelenting. Zarathyn's spells burned through them, each casting a monumental effort. Violet lightning scorched the ground, firestorms swept through the ranks of beasts, and shimmering shields deflected their frenzied attacks. But it wasn't enough. For every monstrosity incinerated, twice as many surged forward, their claws rending the earth as they pushed closer to the rift's beacon of unholy power.

The rift itself throbbed, alive with a malevolent will. It pulsed in defiance of the archmage's efforts, clawing at the fabric of existence with jagged tendrils of green light that split the sky. Its resistance grew stronger, as if it knew Zarathyn's strength was ebbing.

His knees buckled, the weight of his own magic crashing down on him like an iron chain. Zarathyn stumbled, catching himself on his staff. The crystal at its tip, once glowing with brilliant light, now flickered weakly, its power nearly spent. His hands trembled as they gripped the staff, his knuckles white and bloodied. The air burned in his lungs, each breath ragged and shallow.

Around him lay the butchered remains of the knights who had fought so valiantly by his side. Their swords, broken and bloodied, lay in lifeless hands. Their shields, torn apart by claws and acid, were scattered like forgotten relics. He had fought with them, for them, and now they were gone. Only he remained, standing against the impossible.

The creatures were closing in. Their howls tore through the battlefield, a discordant symphony of hunger and rage. Zarathyn straightened, his body protesting with every movement. Blood trickled from his nose, a harbinger of the toll his magic had taken. Yet he raised his staff once more, a defiant snarl curling his lips.

But he knew the truth. He could not hold them back forever. The rift would remain open, spilling its unending tide into the world, consuming everything he had ever fought to protect.

"I must end this," he muttered, the words a

mere breath against the storm of chaos.

The spell came to him unbidden, ancient and forbidden, etched into his mind from a time before mortals dared to play with the threads of reality. To power it would demand more than mana, more than strength—it would take him. All of him. His life force would fuel the spell, and in doing so, sever his thread from the tapestry of existence.

"I give... myself," Zarathyn whispered, his voice trembling with resolve.

The incantation spilled from his lips, each word a dagger of pain that lanced through his body. The air around him ignited with raw energy, the earth splitting beneath his feet. The crystal atop his staff flared violently, cracks spidering across its surface as it drank deeply of his essence.

The agony hit him like a tidal wave. His veins burned, his muscles locked, and his bones felt as though they were being ground to dust. The spell was tearing him apart, drawing the very fabric of his being into itself. Zarathyn gritted his teeth, his vision blurring as waves of nausea and searing pain wracked his body. He wavered, but his hands remained steady on the staff, his focus unbroken.

The creatures, sensing the shift, screamed in unison. They surged forward in a final, desperate attempt to stop him. Tendrils of green light lashed out from the rift, striking at him like whips of molten energy. One tore through his shoulder, leaving a smoldering wound, but Zarathyn did not falter.

The crystal atop his staff shattered.

A blinding wave of pure energy erupted outward, the sound deafening. It slammed into the horde, vaporizing them in an instant. Their twisted forms dissolved into nothingness, their screams snuffed out as the wave consumed them. The ground quaked violently as the rift screamed, its edges folding inward like a collapsing star.

Zarathyn's body disintegrated piece by piece, each fragment of his essence feeding the spell. His flesh burned away, leaving behind a figure of shimmering light, radiant and terrible to behold. Even as his physical form was consumed, his voice remained, the final words of his spell echoing across the battlefield like the toll of a great bell.

The rift imploded. It collapsed into a single, blinding point of light, its desperate tendrils clawing at the air one last time before vanishing. Silence fell as the rift winked out of existence, leaving only a faint shimmer where it had torn reality apart.

When the light faded, the battlefield was unrecognizable. The earth was scorched black, the air heavy with ash and death. The bodies of the knights, already broken, were charred and motionless, their noble sacrifice marked only by the faint gleam of their melted armor.

Zarathyn was gone.

The staff lay in ruins, its splinters scattered among the wreckage. The power that had been him—his essence, his soul—was no more. But somewhere, deep in the void where the rift had been, something stirred. A whisper, faint and chilling, drifted through the emptiness.

Zarathyn's sacrifice had saved the kingdom. But his victory had not gone unnoticed.

CHAPTER 2

Kalen's frail body jerked upright, a gasp tearing from his throat like it had been yanked out. His back screamed with pain, muscles tight and brittle like overused cords. The midday sun bore down mercilessly, baking his sweat into a gritty layer on his skin. His cracked, dirt-encrusted hands barely clung to the splintered shaft of a rusted hoe, the wood worn smooth in some places and jagged in others where the grain had frayed and split. A ragged strip of cloth wrapped around the handle kept the tool from snapping in half, though it felt like it could give out at any moment.

The fields stretched out around him, vast and unforgiving, a sea of desolation. The soil was as dry as bone, riddled with deep cracks that snaked through the earth like scars. No sign of green, no whisper of life. Just dust, and more dust, swirling sluggishly whenever the faintest breeze dared to blow. The other workers were little more than hunched shadows, bent low, hacking at the stubborn ground with tools no better than his own. Their faces, gaunt and hollow, spoke of lives spent fighting battles they could never win.

The air hung thick and oppressive, the kind of heat that sucked the strength out of your bones. Smog drifted low and heavy, shrouding the sky in a mottled gray blanket. Somewhere above, the sun fought to break through, casting the world in a sickly yellow glow that made the landscape feel even more alien. Each breath was a struggle. The fumes bit at Kalen's throat, making his chest ache with every wheezing inhale. The scent of metal, grease, and sweat saturated everything, leaving no room for anything clean or pure.

And then there were the Overseers.

The hulking machines stomped along the edges of the fields, their enormous legs grinding into the dirt with ruthless precision. Their joints hissed and groaned, steam venting from metal exhausts in sharp bursts. The glow of their cores— deep red and pulsing like heartbeats—cut through the smog like an ominous warning. Runes, barely legible under layers of grime, crawled along their iron hides, crackling faintly with a perverse, corrupted energy. Each step they took sent tremors through the ground, a constant reminder of their watchful presence.

Kalen staggered as the vibrations rattled his weakened frame. His knees buckled for a moment, but he managed to keep upright, leaning heavily on the hoe like it was the only thing keeping him tethered to this wretched world. His mind felt fractured, like shards of glass scattered across a stone floor. Memories flitted through his head

—brief, disjointed flashes of fields, Overseers, and faceless overseers shouting orders. The familiar misery of a peasant's life pressed down on him like a weight he had carried for years.

But then, something else.

A force surged within him, wild and alien, clawing its way to the surface. It wasn't Kalen. It wasn't the meek, beaten-down boy who had lived and suffered in this body. It was something far older, far greater.

Zarathyn.

The name erupted in his mind, dragging a tidal wave of ancient memories in its wake. Battles fought beneath burning skies. Words of power, spoken with enough force to shatter mountains. Armies kneeling before him, trembling in awe and terror. The rush of magic, pure and untamed, coursing through his veins like liquid fire.

Kalen's legs gave out, and he crumpled into the dirt, his hoe clattering to the ground beside him. His chest heaved as the flood of memories threatened to overwhelm him, drowning the feeble remnants of Kalen's life under the sheer magnitude of Zarathyn's existence.

His muscles seized violently, his fingers curling into the dusty earth as if trying to anchor himself. Around him, the other workers paused, their weary gazes flicking toward the commotion. A few muttered curses under their breath. One man—bony and sharp-eyed, with a permanent sneer etched into his face—tossed a clod of dirt at

Kalen's trembling form.

"Get up, Kalen," the man growled, his voice as rough as the ground they worked on. "The Overseer sees you lying around, it'll grind you into mulch."

The other workers quickly turned back to their labor, their hunched figures moving in rhythm with the Overseer's looming presence. No one spared him a second glance. No one offered a hand.

But Kalen—or Zarathyn—wasn't paying attention to them anymore. He was lost in the storm raging inside his mind, the fragile walls of Kalen's identity crumbling under the relentless force of Zarathyn's return. The great archmage who had once shaped the world with his will now found himself trapped in a body too frail to contain his power, in a world where the magic he once commanded had been reduced to little more than myth.

The pain was excruciating, but within it was a spark—a promise.

Zarathyn wasn't done. Not by a long shot.

Zarathyn groaned as he forced his frail body upright, the splintered hoe trembling under his weight. Each movement sent sharp jolts through Kalen's untrained muscles, his body protesting the effort like a rusted machine on the verge of breaking down. His breath came in shallow gasps, rattling in his chest as he steadied himself. His fingers tightened on the rough wood, the hoe barely sturdy enough to serve as a makeshift crutch.

He scanned the horizon, his gaze—Kalen's gaze —sweeping over the desolation that stretched endlessly before him. The fields were barren, the soil cracked and lifeless, more dust than earth. But it wasn't just the land that struck him; it was the oppressive weight of the sky above. Massive iron towers pierced the horizon like jagged spears, their chimneys vomiting thick plumes of black smoke that coiled upward and spread like a poison. The sunlight struggled against it, reduced to pale, flickering streaks that bathed the world in a sickly glow.

Zarathyn squinted, his sharp mind—once accustomed to sights of wonder and terror— grappling with the bleakness. This wasn't his world. It wasn't even a twisted shadow of it. This was something entirely alien, a place where magic had been suffocated under the relentless grind of steel and industry.

Strange machines crawled across the land, their iron forms groaning and clanking with mechanical malice. Gears turned with grinding precision, their teeth slick with grease. Steam hissed from vents, mingling with the smoke to create an air thick enough to choke on. The machines weren't merely tools; they were predators, devouring the land beneath their massive iron claws. Some dragged serrated plows that tore through the earth with brutal efficiency, while others hauled wagons filled with ore, debris, or worse—human bodies too broken to continue working.

Workers trudged in the machines' shadow, their figures hunched and beaten. Their movements were mechanical, lifeless, like puppets on strings pulled too tight. Zarathyn could see the exhaustion etched into every line of their bodies, the dull hopelessness in their eyes. None of them looked up. None of them paused. To stop was to die, and they all knew it.

But it was the Overseer's mech that commanded his attention.

The monstrous construct loomed over the field, a hulking mass of iron and death. Its frame bristled with weaponry—spiked harpoons, rotating blades, and serrated cannons, each more horrific than the last. Its legs were impossibly thick, stomping into the earth with a weight that sent tremors through the ground. Each step ground rocks into dust, its metal feet sinking deep into the soil, crushing what little life remained.

A faint pulse of light flickered from its chest, a steady, unnatural rhythm that felt far too familiar. Zarathyn's breath hitched. The mech was powered by something he couldn't mistake.

Magic.

But this wasn't the vibrant, untamed energy he had once commanded. This was magic twisted, corrupted, enslaved. Its very essence felt wrong, like a wolf wearing chains. The runes etched into the mech's frame shimmered faintly, their patterns crude and jagged, a perverse mimicry of the delicate spellwork he had once woven. This was a bastardization of everything he had stood for, a mockery of the power he had once wielded.

Rage flared in his chest, hot and unrelenting. His knuckles whitened around the hoe's shaft as he steadied himself, his legs trembling but unyielding. Kalen's body wasn't strong enough for this. It wasn't meant for resistance or rebellion. But Zarathyn wasn't Kalen, and he never would be.

He forced himself to look closer at the workers. Their hands were bloodied and raw, some missing fingers, others with deep, jagged scars that spoke of punishments far worse than any man should endure. A young boy, barely more than a child, stumbled under the weight of a metal crate. The mech's glowing eyes locked onto him, and a low, grinding whir signaled its intent.

Before Zarathyn could even think to move, the mech's spiked harpoon shot out with brutal speed. It impaled the boy through the chest, lifting him off the ground like a broken doll. Blood sprayed across the dry earth in a violent arc, the crimson stark against the endless gray. The boy's body hung limp for a moment before the harpoon retracted, dragging him into the mech's grinding maw.

The workers didn't flinch. They didn't cry out. They just kept moving, their heads bowed, their hands working.

Zarathyn's stomach churned, his anger

bubbling hotter, fiercer. This was the world he had died to save? This twisted, hollow existence? The thought of his sacrifice—his life, his power—leading to this made his blood boil.

His trembling fingers dug into the splintered wood of the hoe. His mind raced, Zarathyn's memories weaving through Kalen's like threads in a tapestry. He couldn't stay silent. He wouldn't. But before he could even begin to think of a plan, the Overseer's mech turned.

Its glowing eyes locked onto him.

The shock hit him like a hammer. Magic. It was faint, distant—like a dying ember smothered under wet ash. But it was there. The sensation clawed at him, almost like a familiar scent carried on the wind. His mind screamed for the power, the vast force he had once wielded without thought, but nothing came. His sacrifice had saved the kingdom—he had thought that was enough —but now, looking at the horizon of this new, unrecognizable world, it felt like that sacrifice had merely planted a seed for something darker.

His lips curled into a grimace, rage seething beneath his skin. He couldn't believe it. He had died to save his people, to save the world—and now this? This... wasteland? His fingers gripped the hoe tighter, splinters biting into his hands, but the pain didn't matter. The world around him had changed. He could feel it in every dry breath he took, every footstep that churned the soil beneath him.

The air, thick with suffocating heat, made his chest ache. He wasn't sure if the burning in his lungs was from the sun or something else. Something deeper. The ground beneath him felt unnatural—cracked, dry, as if even the earth had been drained of life. The workers around him—these strange, gaunt people—moved in robotic, synchronized motions. Their eyes, hollow and vacant, scanned the horizon, avoiding any semblance of thought.

He tried to focus. What is this place?

His body betrayed him with every step. His legs wobbled like a child learning to walk, each movement foreign, sluggish. His breath came in short, desperate gasps. I am trapped. The body he inhabited was weak—too weak—and yet somehow, he could feel the power within him, faint, muted, as if it were being held back by some unseen force. His memories were fractured. They were there, deep within him, but they were distant. The flood of them had been too much, too fast. This wasn't the world he had known. This wasn't the world he had fought for.

He looked to the horizon. And that's when he saw it. The massive iron towers stretching toward the sky, blotting out the sun. Smoke, thick and black, billowed from them, choking the air. The air itself tasted wrong. Not like the crisp, clean winds of his homeland, but thick with something burning—something unnatural. And those... things, crawling over the land, moving in jerky, mechanical motions—these were no creatures. They were machines, their joints grinding with a rhythmic precision that sent a chill down his spine.

Zarathyn tried to force his body upright, but his knees buckled again. His mind was sharp—too sharp for this body, this vessel. He could feel the stirrings of magic, so faint, so suffocated by the weight of the world, but it was there. I must... He reached for it, tried to grasp it. But the magic recoiled, as if it, too, had been caged, imprisoned. What has happened?

The people around him moved like shadows, their faces sunken and devoid of expression, their bodies bent under the weight of unseen chains. He saw one man, his back hunched in a permanent bow, his eyes dull, his hands moving mechanically. As he looked closer, Zarathyn saw the Overseer's mech in the distance—massive and looming. It towered over the workers like a monstrous shadow, its glowing eyes scanning the fields.

And then, the sick realization hit. The Overseer... it was alive, and yet it wasn't. It was something else. Its glowing eyes, cold and unblinking, bore down on him, its metallic frame shifting, its hum resonating in the very bones of the earth. Something about it felt wrong. Wrong in a way that he couldn't quite place.

The workers didn't even look up. They were too far gone to notice the presence of this towering machine, too broken to resist. But Zarathyn knew.

He knew that whatever this place was, it was built on something twisted. The same magic he had once harnessed and used to bend the world to his will was now a forgotten relic, hidden beneath layers of rust and stone.

The rage burned deeper now. It roared in his chest, a fire he could no longer control. His fingers dug into the hoe, and he forced his legs to move again, staggering, but moving. He couldn't afford to collapse, not now. Not when everything was so... wrong. He didn't know how, or why, but this was his new reality. This was where he had awoken, and this was where he had to survive.

Zarathyn's mind spun, every thought colliding in a blur of confusion, but there was one thing that he knew for certain: this world—whatever it had become—wasn't what he had left behind. And he would find out why. Even if it meant crawling through the dirt, he would claw his way back to power. He would uncover the truth of this broken land.

For now, he gritted his teeth and kept working, his hands moving mechanically, as if he too were becoming one of the mindless shadows around him. But deep within him, something burned— something more than just the need for survival. A spark. A whisper. He wasn't done yet. Not by a long shot.

CHAPTER 3

Nightfall draped the fields in darkness, but it brought no mercy. The cloying smog from the iron towers hung heavy in the air, thick and sour, clinging to skin like an oily second layer. The peasants shuffled toward the barracks, their movements mechanical, their shoulders hunched as though the weight of their lives pressed down on them. Zarathyn followed, his legs dragging through the dust, every step an exercise in humiliation. He, who had once strode through halls of marble and summoned the heavens to his will, now stumbled into a hovel fit for cattle.

The barracks were a long, sagging structure of rotting wood and rusted nails, the faint stench of mildew and unwashed bodies pouring out before the door even opened. Inside, the dirt floor was pounded hard from years of restless feet, the thin, patchy straw scattered across it doing nothing to mask the damp cold seeping up from below. Shadows clung to the corners, thick and oppressive, as the only light came from a dying ember in a single iron brazier.

Zarathyn's body screamed with pain as he

dropped onto one of the splintered wooden bunks lining the walls. The mattress, if it could even be called that, was nothing more than a sack of lumpy straw, stinking of sweat and mold. His muscles trembled, his back ached, and his hands burned from the countless blisters raised by the unforgiving handle of the hoe. He stared down at them—raw, cracked, streaked with grime—and clenched his fists. His anger, his indignation, simmered beneath the surface. I was a king. A god among men. And now I am… this?

The others filed in, silent as phantoms. They avoided each other's gazes, heads bowed, bodies folding in on themselves like they were trying to disappear. None spoke. None dared. The air was thick with fear, not just of the Overseers but of something more insidious—a resignation so deep it felt alive, a parasite gnawing at the edges of their humanity.

In the farthest corner, an old man sat slumped against the wall, his leg twisted at an unnatural angle, as useless as the battered tin cup beside him. He muttered to himself, his voice low and gravelly, the words catching on his breath like pebbles in a stream. Zarathyn's ears pricked up. He focused, narrowing in on the sounds.

It wasn't nonsense.

The words were fractured, stilted, like a broken melody, but they were unmistakable: the echoes of an incantation. Old magic. Poorly woven, poorly spoken, but there. Zarathyn pushed himself upright, ignoring the protests of his battered body, and moved toward the man.

"You," he said, his voice cutting through the oppressive silence like a blade.

The old man's muttering stopped. He looked up, his milky eyes narrowing, his lips pressed into a thin, cracked line. He didn't speak.

"Where did you learn that?" Zarathyn demanded, his tone sharper now.

The man recoiled like a beaten dog, his gnarled hands clutching at the cup beside him as if it might somehow shield him. Around them, the other peasants stiffened. Heads turned away, shoulders hunched tighter, as though pretending not to hear might save them from whatever storm Zarathyn was about to bring.

A woman on the next bunk hissed through her teeth, her voice barely above a whisper. "Shut your mouth. Don't draw attention, fool." She shot him a glare, her gaunt face etched with desperation. "The Overseers hear everything."

Zarathyn turned toward her, his jaw tightening. "Let them hear," he said coldly, though he couldn't help the flicker of unease that twisted in his gut.

But she shook her head violently, her sunken eyes wide with panic. "You don't know what you're saying." Her gaze darted toward the slatted walls, as if expecting them to burst open at any moment. "They'll come for all of us."

The room fell even quieter, the kind of silence

that suffocates. Zarathyn looked back at the old man, whose lips had pressed together in a firm line. His hands trembled, clutching his pathetic tin cup as if it were a lifeline. The faint echoes of the incantation lingered in Zarathyn's mind, teasing him with half-formed images of runes and rituals. It was crude, yes. Pathetic even. But it was magic. Real magic. And in this desolate place, that meant something.

"Where," Zarathyn repeated, his voice a low growl, "did you learn it?"

The old man shook his head, slow and deliberate, his milky eyes filling with something like fear. Or was it defiance?

Before Zarathyn could press further, a distant metallic groan echoed through the air, sending a shiver down his spine. The others froze. Every head turned toward the sound, and the woman beside him clutched her chest like her heart might leap from it.

The Overseer.

Its heavy, deliberate footsteps sent vibrations through the ground, growing louder with every second. Clang. Clang. Clang. Each step was a death knell, the sound of inevitability marching closer.

"Fool," the woman whispered harshly, her voice trembling. "You might have doomed us all."

Zarathyn stood rigid, his mind racing. He had been a lord of magic once, a warrior who had faced down armies and gods alike. But here, in this frail body, surrounded by cowards, with no power to call upon, he felt—if only for a moment—like prey.

The clang of footsteps drew closer, steady as a heartbeat, their weight rattling loose splinters from the barracks walls. Zarathyn sat rigid, his body betraying none of the tension coiled in his chest. Around him, the peasants had shrunk into themselves, their heads bowed, their trembling forms blending into the shadows.

The steps stopped outside the barracks, and for a long, dreadful moment, there was nothing but silence. Even the rustling of the wind seemed to hold its breath. Then came the low whine of metal shifting, the hiss of pistons, and the splintering groan of wood as the door creaked open.

The Overseer loomed in the doorway, its hulking frame framed by the faint green glow of its visor. The machine ducked slightly to fit its bulk into the narrow space, its claws curling into the doorframe as it leaned inside.

The green light swept over the room in a slow, deliberate arc. Zarathyn's skin prickled as it passed over him, the faint hum of energy from the Overseer's core vibrating in his chest. The peasants stiffened, their gazes fixed firmly on the floor. One man let out a quiet whimper before clamping his hand over his mouth.

The Overseer's light didn't waver. It moved from face to face, lingering for a moment before shifting to the next. When it reached Zarathyn, it stopped.

The hum deepened, resonating like the growl

of a beast testing its prey. The machine tilted its head, as if puzzled, its visor flaring brighter. Zarathyn felt its scrutiny, cold and clinical, as though it could see far beyond his frail form and into something deeper.

He didn't lower his gaze. If this machine wanted to study him, he would meet it head-on. His lips pressed into a thin line, his expression unreadable, though every nerve in his body screamed at him to bow, to cower like the others.

The Overseer shifted, stepping fully into the room now. Its clawed feet sank into the dirt floor, leaving deep gouges in its wake. It stood over Zarathyn, its bulk casting a shadow that seemed to swallow the flickering light entirely.

"Move," someone hissed behind him, their voice barely audible. But Zarathyn didn't. He couldn't.

The Overseer crouched, lowering its head until its visor was level with Zarathyn's face. The green light was blinding now, so bright it painted everything in sickly hues. He felt the machine's presence pressing down on him, cold and suffocating.

Then it struck.

The movement was so fast that Zarathyn barely registered it. A clawed hand lashed out, its metal edge slicing a sharp line across his lip. The force of the blow sent him sprawling to the ground, his cheek hitting the dirt hard enough to bruise. The taste of blood filled his mouth, sharp and metallic.

The peasants gasped, a few flinching back into the corners as if they might be next. Zarathyn pushed himself up onto one elbow, spitting blood onto the floor. His head swam, but his eyes remained fixed on the Overseer.

The machine loomed for a moment longer, its claws flexing, as if deciding whether to finish the job. Then, with a faint, mechanical hum, it straightened. It turned away, its movements unnervingly smooth, and stepped out of the barracks.

The room was silent, save for the faint clanking of the Overseer's retreat. When the sound of its footsteps faded into the distance, the tension snapped.

"What's wrong with you?" someone whispered harshly.

Zarathyn didn't answer. He wiped the blood from his lip with the back of his hand, his mind racing. Whatever that thing had seen in him, it hadn't liked it. That much was clear.

And now he had learned something too. These machines were more than lifeless tools. They were watching, studying, and ready to act without hesitation.

It wasn't fear he felt now, though. It was anger. Smoldering, controlled, and focused. This wasn't a body that could fight—not yet. But he had endured worse.

For now, he would wait. He would learn. And

then, when the time came, he would strike.

The barracks settled into an uneasy stillness after the Overseer's departure. The air was thick with sweat and fear, the peasants avoiding even the sound of their own breathing. Zarathyn sat back against the splintered wall, his bruised cheek throbbing, and his split lip sticky with drying blood. He wiped it with the back of his hand, ignoring the ache that radiated through his frail body.

The silence broke with a faint shuffling. At first, Zarathyn thought it was just the wind rattling loose dirt against the walls. Then he noticed a figure crawling toward him, the sound of knobby joints scraping against the packed floor like a slow, deliberate whisper.

It was the old man—the one with the gnarled leg who had been muttering earlier. His milky eyes gleamed faintly in the dim light, his bony hands dragging his wasted body closer with unsettling determination. The others pretended not to notice, turning their faces away and pulling their thin blankets tighter around themselves.

Zarathyn tensed but didn't move. The man was thin to the point of emaciation, but there was something unsettling in his movements—a jittery, insectile energy. The old man's cracked lips parted into a grin, revealing the jagged stumps of yellowed teeth.

"You..." he rasped, his voice raw and broken, barely audible over the sound of his dragging limbs. "You're not the same as before."

Zarathyn's eyes narrowed. "What do you mean?"

The man stopped at his side, propping himself up on one elbow. He leaned in close, too close, his breath reeking of decay and something metallic. His voice dropped even lower, his words a broken whisper that only Zarathyn could hear.

"There's power in you now. Power that wasn't in that boy before." His grin widened, grotesque in the dim light. "I can see it—burning, just under the skin. You're hiding it, but it's there."

Zarathyn stiffened. The man's words sent a chill rippling through him, though he fought to keep his expression blank. This frail peasant could see him—sense him—in a way no ordinary man should.

"What do you know?" Zarathyn asked, his voice sharp but quiet.

The old man chuckled, a wet, rasping sound. "More than I should. I've lived too long, seen too much. The Dominion doesn't like folks like me, you see. Those who remember. They call us mad. They send their Overseers to watch us, to crush us when we talk too much."

The word "Dominion" hung in the air like a thundercloud. Zarathyn's mind latched onto it, dissecting it, turning it over for meaning.

"The Dominion?" he repeated, keeping his tone neutral.

The man nodded, his matted hair falling over

his hollow cheeks. "They own it all. The fields, the air, the sky. Everything. Machines rule now. Big, iron things with no soul. And the magic... oh, the magic's gone. Or so they think. But I know better." He leaned in closer, his voice dropping to a conspiratorial whisper. "The Dominion didn't destroy it. They hoard it. Lock it away, chain it, bleed it dry to power their monstrosities. You saw it, didn't you? In the Overseer?"

Zarathyn said nothing, but the old man's grin only grew.

"You did," he hissed. "I can see it in your eyes. You've felt it, haven't you? The pulse. The hum. They think they've tamed it, but magic isn't something you can tame. It's alive. It remembers. And now it's found you."

The old man's hand shot out, gnarled fingers gripping Zarathyn's wrist with surprising strength. "Whatever you are, whatever you've brought here, they'll know soon enough. The Overseers watch. The Overseers always watch."

Zarathyn pulled his arm free, his mind racing. This "Dominion" controlled the world through machines and imprisoned magic, remnants of a power that once thrived under his rule. But how long had it been? How much had changed?

The old man laughed again, softer this time, his grip loosening as he slumped back to the floor. "Be careful, stranger," he whispered, his voice already fading. "The Dominion doesn't like ripples in their pond. And you... oh, you're a storm."

The man collapsed into a heap, his chest rising and falling with labored breaths. Around them, the barracks remained silent, the other peasants pretending not to have heard a word.

Zarathyn sat still, his mind spinning. He glanced at the doorway where the Overseer had stood moments ago, its cold green light scanning the room. The old man was right about one thing. If they didn't know who he was yet, it wouldn't take long.

CHAPTER 4

The next day arrived with no ceremony—just the same choking air and the same sickly yellow sun barely cutting through the smog. Zarathyn —trapped in Kalen's frail, aching body—forced himself upright as the Overseer's horn blared, dragging the peasants out of their restless sleep. The barracks emptied like a sluggish tide, bodies moving in silence toward the fields.

Zarathyn gripped the hoe with trembling hands, its splintered handle rough against his calloused palms. Every swing of the tool sent jolts of pain through his thin arms, his muscles screaming for rest. But he kept at it, his sharp eyes scanning the landscape as he worked.

The Overseer's mech stalked the edge of the field like a predator, its massive iron frame groaning with every calculated step. The pulsing glow of its core was faint but unmistakable— a twisted mockery of the magic Zarathyn had once wielded. The peasants moved in frightened silence, their gazes pinned to the ground, but Zarathyn caught the flickers of something more. A hurried glance exchanged between two workers. A whispered word too soft to catch. A furtive nod. It wasn't much, but it was there: sparks.

As the sun dipped low, turning the sky into a canvas of muddied reds and yellows, the air shifted. A commotion erupted at the far end of the field. Zarathyn straightened, his grip tightening on the hoe as he squinted toward the noise.

A young woman stood alone, her head high and her fists clenched. Her frame was wiry, but she held herself with the kind of defiance that didn't bend easily. Her name rippled through the workers in murmurs: Lira. Zarathyn didn't need to ask what had happened—her torn satchel and the spilled handful of dried bread at her feet told the story. She had stolen rations.

The Overseer's mech hissed as it halted. The machine's hulking form bent forward, releasing a figure from its chest—its pilot. The Overseer descended, his polished armor catching the last rays of sunlight. His face was obscured by a mask, but his posture spoke volumes. This was no administrator, no manager of men. This was an enforcer. A soldier.

The peasants froze where they stood, every one of them rooted in fear. Lira didn't move. She stared the Overseer down, her eyes blazing with a fire that no amount of suffering had extinguished.

The Overseer wasted no time. His steel-plated fist shot forward, cracking against her jaw with a sickening thud. Lira crumpled like a snapped reed, blood spilling from her split lip onto the parched earth.

Zarathyn's vision blurred with rage. His hands trembled around the hoe, his knuckles white. Every instinct screamed at him to act, to lash out, to tear the Overseer apart. But his body was a husk, his power caged, and he knew it. He ground his teeth until his jaw ached, forcing himself to stand still as the Overseer bent down, grabbed Lira by her arm, and dragged her toward the mech. Her cries cut through the field like jagged glass, raw and desperate, before fading into the mechanical hum of the machine.

The peasants resumed their work with heads bowed, their silence heavier than before. Zarathyn couldn't move. His chest heaved with fury and shame, the air burning in his lungs. He stood there as the last light bled from the sky, his grip on the hoe so tight it felt like it might snap.

That night, as the barracks settled into a restless, fearful quiet, Zarathyn stared at the wooden slats of the ceiling. His cheek still ached where the Overseer had struck him the night before, but he barely felt it now. All he could see was Lira's defiant face, her blood staining the earth, and the monstrous machine dragging her away.

He made his vow in the dark, his whispered words barely audible even to himself. "No more."

This Dominion had stolen everything—his world, his power, his name. They had taken a kingdom forged from storms and reduced it to this... to chains, to smog, to blood spilled in fields of ash. But he was still here. Still breathing. And he would reclaim it all, piece by broken piece.

They would feel his rage. They would see their empire burn.

***

In the days that followed, Zarathyn—trapped in the frail husk of Kalen—pushed himself harder than any whip ever could. Not with the hoe or the backbreaking labor demanded by the Overseer, but in the quiet corners of the barracks, in the stolen moments when the watchful mech's glow dimmed and the workers' snores filled the night air. He tested the boundaries of this fragile shell, prodding and stretching, searching for the faintest flicker of what he'd once commanded.

The first night, he sat cross-legged on the barracks' dirt floor, his hands trembling as he focused. The air around him felt dead, suffocated by the Dominion's machines, but deep beneath the surface—buried under layers of grime and rust—he sensed a thread of something. It was thin, fragile as a spider's web, but it was there. Magic. Twisted and wounded, like a bird with broken wings, but alive.

He concentrated, closing his borrowed eyes, letting his breath slow. His fingers moved in a pattern he had etched into memory centuries ago, tracing sigils that once summoned tempests. Now, they barely stirred the air. At first, there was nothing but the cold press of failure. Then, a flicker. A spark no larger than an ember danced in his palm before fizzling into nothing.

It was pathetic. Humbling. But it was enough.

By the second night, the ember grew into a tiny pulse of light, weak but steady, like the last gasp of a dying star. Zarathyn gritted his teeth, his concentration razor-sharp. The effort sent a wave of nausea rolling through him, but he refused to stop. He willed the light to shift, to stretch. Slowly, it obeyed, elongating into a thread of gold before vanishing into the stale air.

Every muscle in Kalen's pitiful body screamed in protest, but Zarathyn didn't care. That thread of gold—it was more than he had expected. Proof that even in this wretched form, even in this ruined world, his magic was not entirely lost.

The third night, he dared to go further. He crouched low in the shadowed corner of the barracks, away from prying eyes, and tried to manipulate the air itself. His hands moved in deliberate arcs, commanding the faint currents of the stale atmosphere. For long, agonizing moments, nothing happened. Then, a whisper—a faint stir of wind brushed his cheek. It was barely perceptible, but it was enough to send his pulse racing.

The old man, who had taken to muttering his nonsense from the far side of the barracks, caught sight of Zarathyn's efforts. Crawling closer like a broken insect, his milky eyes gleamed with something other than madness. "Yer stirrin' the unseen," he rasped, his voice low and uneven.

Zarathyn didn't respond. He was too focused, his hands weaving through invisible currents as he willed the air to move. The old man crept closer, his gnarled fingers reaching out to hover near Zarathyn's. "Didn't think it could still be done," he muttered. "The Dominion squeezed it all dry. Left the world bleedin', but you... you got somethin'. Somethin' that don't belong here."

Zarathyn snapped his eyes open and fixed the man with a hard glare. "Explain yourself," he hissed.

The old man flinched but didn't retreat. Instead, he leaned in closer, his breath reeking of decay and stale rations. "The Dominion," he began, his voice barely above a whisper. "They took it all —the magic, the life, the old ways. Smashed it into gears and wires, locked it away in their machines. But you... there's a fire in you, boy. A fire that ain't been lit in centuries."

Zarathyn's lip curled. "What do you know of fire, old man? You barely cling to life yourself."

The man grinned, a toothless, feral expression. "More than you think. Saw it, years ago—what little was left. They've been huntin' it ever since, squeezin' it outta relics, hoardin' what they can't burn. That's what powers their beasts, boy. That glow in their machines? That's our lifeblood. That's magic, twisted and chained."

Zarathyn's mind raced. He thought of the

Overseer's mech, the faint pulsing core that reeked of bound energy. It made sense now, in a sick, twisted way. The Dominion hadn't killed magic outright. They had enslaved it.

"And the people?" Zarathyn asked, his voice low, dangerous. "Do they know what's been stolen from them?"

The old man chuckled darkly. "They don't even remember it existed. Just stories now, bedtime tales for the desperate. But you... you could remind 'em. If yer careful. If yer smart."

Zarathyn narrowed his eyes, his thoughts churning. He wasn't ready—not yet. His power was a mere flicker of what it once was, and his body was a weak, trembling vessel. But the old man was right about one thing: the fire was still there, buried deep, waiting to be unleashed.

"Keep your voice down," Zarathyn ordered, his tone sharp. "And don't speak of this again—not to anyone."

The old man nodded, his grin fading into a solemn expression. "Yer the first spark I've seen in a long time, boy. Don't let it go out."

Zarathyn turned away, his hands still trembling with exhaustion. He didn't need the old man's encouragement. The Dominion had stolen his world, corrupted the magic he once ruled, and turned his sacrifice into a mockery.

He would remind them. All of them. But first, he needed strength. The fire might be faint, but it was far from extinguished. And when it roared to life again, the Dominion would burn.

CHAPTER 5

The Overseer's mech stood like an iron sentinel in the fields, its glowing core pulsing with a faint hum that seeped into every corner of Zarathyn's mind. The machine radiated dominion, a monument to the empire's stranglehold on magic. Zarathyn—no, Kalen, he reminded himself —kept his head low, the worn handle of his hoe digging into his blistered palms as he worked. But his eyes tracked the mech's every movement, and his mind churned with quiet fury.

He had spent the last days weaving scraps of power, testing his limits when no one was looking. Tonight, he would act. The workers wouldn't rise on their own, too broken by years of oppression to imagine rebellion. But they would follow a spark if it caught fire.

As the sun reached its peak, casting long, jagged shadows across the cracked dirt, Kalen began his incantation. His lips moved soundlessly, the ancient words spilling out in a rhythm that felt almost foreign to his tongue. The spell was crude, slapped together with the scraps of knowledge he'd salvaged in this ruined world. It wasn't elegant, but it didn't need to be. It just needed to hurt.

The ground beneath the mech trembled. At first, it was subtle—a faint shudder that could have been dismissed as nothing more than the earth settling. Then came the crack. It was sharp and sudden, like the snap of dry bone, and the earth split beneath the machine's massive weight. One of its spindly, steel legs plunged into the opening, the core above it flickering erratically like a dying lantern.

Shouts rang out from the Overseer, his voice a metallic bark amplified by the mech's speakers. "Hold the line!" he roared, his tone laced with fury. The workers froze, their hands clutching tools that now seemed pitiful in the face of the Dominion's wrath.

Kalen seized the moment. "Now!" he bellowed, his voice cutting through the chaos. "Run! Fight!"

For a heartbeat, nothing happened. Then, like floodwaters breaking through a dam, the field erupted into chaos. Workers bolted in every direction, some racing for the safety of the distant woods, others flinging stones, broken tools, and clumps of dirt at the crippled mech. It wasn't organized, but it was defiance, raw and untamed.

The Overseer slammed his fists against the controls of his mech, trying to wrench it free from the earth's grasp. The machine groaned in protest, gears grinding as its core surged brighter. Sparks flew from the damaged limb, showering the nearest workers with molten metal. A few screamed, clutching burned skin, but others kept throwing, driven by a rage they hadn't known they possessed.

Kalen felt a savage burst of triumph. For the first time, the Dominion's symbol of power wasn't invincible. It bled, it faltered. But that triumph soured quickly.

The soldiers came.

They stormed the fields with relentless precision, moving as a pack of trained predators. The sun, sinking low on the horizon, painted their steel armor in shades of gold and crimson, a mockery of the blood they were about to spill. Their blades gleamed like fangs, sharp and eager, and their boots churned the dry soil into a haze of dust as they closed in on the scattered workers.

The first peasant, a wiry man with nothing but a rusted sickle in hand, let out a desperate cry and charged. His voice cracked as he swung wildly, aiming for the nearest soldier. It was over before it began. The soldier sidestepped with mechanical ease, his sword arcing downward in a single, fluid motion. The blade bit deep into the man's neck, severing flesh and muscle with a sickening crunch. He crumpled to the ground, blood pooling around his twitching body, staining the earth a deep, glistening red.

Another worker, a young boy barely old enough to wield the wooden hoe he carried, stepped forward in blind fury. His face twisted with rage as he raised the tool high, but he never got the chance to bring it down. The blunt end of a soldier's spear slammed into his temple with a sharp crack, sending him sprawling to the dirt. His skull collapsed inward, a grotesque dent marring his lifeless face. Blood and brain matter seeped into the soil as the spear's wielder yanked it back, his expression unmoved.

The Overseer stood on the sidelines, his silhouette framed by the hulking remains of his mech. He had abandoned the crippled machine, climbing free of its cockpit as chaos erupted. His face, streaked with dirt and sweat, twisted into a grotesque mask of rage. Veins bulged along his neck as he barked commands, his voice cutting through the screams and the clang of steel like a whip. "No mercy! Drive them down!"

He jabbed a finger toward a cluster of fleeing peasants, his movements sharp and precise. Soldiers pivoted at his orders, splitting off to pursue their prey with ruthless efficiency. The Overseer's lips curled into a snarl as he watched the slaughter unfold, his eyes gleaming with a dark satisfaction.

Kalen didn't hesitate. He dropped his hoe and bolted, his weak body trembling with effort as he sprinted toward the treeline. Behind him, the screams of the workers filled the air, mingling with the guttural war cries of the soldiers. He didn't look back. He couldn't.

By the time he stumbled into the forest, his

legs were shaking so violently he could barely stand. He collapsed beneath a gnarled oak, gasping for breath as the sounds of slaughter faded behind him. His lip was split, his cheek bruised where the Overseer had struck him earlier, but the pain felt distant, unimportant.

He clenched his fists, his nails digging into his palms until they drew blood. This wasn't over. This wasn't defeat.

The Dominion had shown its strength today, but so had he. They had taken his world, his power, and now they sought to claim his spirit. But they hadn't reckoned with him.

"Piece by piece," he whispered to himself, his voice a low growl. "I'll take it all back. And from this day hence I shall never again think of myself as Kalen, for I am Zarathyn, and the world will learn to tremble at the sound of my name."

His body ached, his magic was still a fragile ember, but he could feel the fire stirring deep within. Tonight was only the beginning. The Dominion would bleed for what they had done. And one day, the world would remember what it meant to be free.

CHAPTER 6

Zarathyn trudged down the cracked dirt path, each step heavier than the last. His legs burned from days of relentless walking, and his ribs ached where the Dominion guards had beaten him during his escape. The loose, ill-fitting rags clinging to his gaunt frame did little to shield him from the chill in the air. Still, he pressed on. His name, once spoken with reverence and fear, now clung to him like a promise.

Zarathyn.

He would rise again.

The village crept into Zarathyn's view as he staggered around the bend, a hollow, sagging thing that barely clung to existence. What passed for homes were little more than heaps of rotted timber, slapped together with tarps that flapped weakly in the wind and mud caked thick in the gaps. Roofs sagged inward under their own weight, riddled with gaps so wide the sky poured through in jagged, mocking beams of light. The place seemed to recoil from itself, as though ashamed of what it had become.

Zarathyn's jaw clenched as he stopped at the

edge of the barren fields, his gaze dragging across the desolate landscape. The sight was painfully familiar. This was the Dominion's handiwork. Not a labor camp like the one he had escaped, where overseers cracked whips and barked orders under the shadow of their looming mechs, driving prisoners to their limits. No, this was something quieter but just as insidious—a peasant village wrung dry by endless taxes and neglect.

Here, there were no iron fences or guards with spears, no mechs stomping through the dust to enforce Dominion law. The village didn't need chains or threats to keep its people in line. Hunger did the job well enough. The faces in the fields told the story plainly: hollowed eyes, sunken cheeks, backs permanently hunched under the weight of desperation. They toiled not under whips but under the crushing inevitability of starvation.

The faint memory of the Overseer's mech drifted back to Zarathyn, unbidden. The mechanical beast's hum still seemed to rattle faintly in the back of his skull, a phantom of the days he'd spent slaving under its shadow. He couldn't shake the feeling that it was all part of the same monstrous design—one vast, grinding machine fueled by human misery. The labor camps, the broken villages, the starving peasants —it was all connected.

The Dominion didn't just take what it needed and move on. It took everything. It hollowed out a place, carved away its soul, and left nothing behind but the husk of what once was. Zarathyn tightened his grip on his walking staff, the wood creaking under the strain. Every ounce of him wanted to do something, anything, to stop it. But the same gnawing helplessness he'd felt since his escape dragged at him like iron weights. He had power, yes, but not enough. Not yet.

He stared at the village, his mind racing. This wasn't a camp where prisoners were forced into labor beneath the watchful eyes of guards. This was a place where despair had already done its work, where people broke themselves for the slimmest chance of survival. And the Dominion didn't even need to stand here to keep them shackled. The thought burned in his chest, but he forced himself to take a slow breath. He'd seen what rushing into the jaws of the machine could do. He wasn't going to make that mistake again.

A few thin trails of smoke curled from crooked chimneys, more like dying whispers than signs of life. The air carried the sharp tang of acrid fumes, making Zarathyn's nose sting. Whatever they burned, it wasn't firewood—maybe scraps of damp straw, maybe bits of their own hovels. Definitely not anything that might feed the belly or warm the bones.

Out in the fields, a ragged line of peasants shuffled through the dust. Their backs bent low as they hacked at the lifeless soil with rusted tools that glinted dully under the sun. The earth beneath them was as dead as they looked—gray, cracked, and hostile, splitting apart in deep veins that clawed toward the horizon. It was dirt that hadn't seen rain in months, maybe years. Dirt that had forgotten what it was to give life.

The peasants were little more than moving skeletons, their flesh stretched so tight it looked like their bones might tear through. Their cheeks were sunken hollows, their arms and legs spindly sticks. One woman shuffled along, dragging a broken rake behind her. Her shoulders quaked with effort, each step slower than the last.

In the middle of the field, a boy no older than ten gripped a splintered hoe, the wood too long and too heavy for his thin arms. His head drooped as he leaned against it, shoulders sagging like he bore the weight of the world. Zarathyn stopped walking, watching the boy sway on his feet like a wilted flower caught in a faint breeze.

The boy's knees gave out without warning, and he crumpled face-first into the dirt. A dry cloud puffed around his frail body, the soil clinging to his sweat-streaked skin. He didn't cry out. He didn't even flinch. He just lay there, motionless.

No one ran to his side. No one even paused in their work. The nearest peasant cast a fleeting glance in the boy's direction before bending back to her task, her grip tightening on her rusted hoe. There was no room here for compassion, Zarathyn realized. No strength left for it.

The scene gnawed at him, clawing deep into his chest. He felt the weight of the name he carried, a name that had once commanded armies and bent nations to its will. But here, now, Zarathyn was as powerless as the rest of them. The fire inside him sputtered, caught between fury and helplessness, as he stared at a village choking on the last scraps of its life.

***

The sun hung low in the sky, its dying light casting long shadows over the cracked fields as Zarathyn leaned against his makeshift staff. His body still ached from the days of running, but the kindly farmer who'd offered him a place to stay —Jorek, an older man with broad shoulders and rough, weathered hands—hadn't asked for much in return. "Work for your supper," Jorek had said, handing him a rusted plow that looked older than the village itself. Zarathyn, once a being of untouchable power, had taken it with a nod. He knew better than to scoff at charity now.

The fields were a battlefield of their own, the soil hard as stone, as if the earth itself had given up. Zarathyn pushed the plow, his muscles protesting with every step. Jorek worked alongside him, his movements practiced but heavy with age. The man's ox had died months ago, leaving the farmer to haul the plow himself. Seeing him strain against the harness, Zarathyn silently took the lead, his fingers white-knuckling the cracked wooden handles.

"You've done this before, eh?" Jorek asked, his tone light despite the weight of the task.

"Something like it," Zarathyn lied, his voice steady. The truth was, his hands weren't made for labor. They were meant for wielding power, shaping the fabric of the world itself. Now, they blistered against splintered wood.

Jorek nodded but didn't pry. He seemed content to let the silence settle, the rhythmic scrape of the plow carving shallow furrows into the unyielding earth. Eventually, though, his voice broke through the quiet, tinged with a bitterness that Zarathyn could feel in his bones. "You're lucky you showed up when you did. Another few weeks, and there'd be nothing left to work with. Dominion taxes…" He spat into the dirt. "They'll bleed us dry."

Zarathyn glanced over, his gaze sharp. "Taxes?"

Jorek wiped his brow with a sleeve, his face grim. "Aye. Grain, livestock, coin—whatever they can take, they take it. Say it's for the war effort, but all it does is leave us starving. Refuse, and you're hauled off to the camps. Or worse."

The words hit like a hammer. Zarathyn had seen the "worse." The camps weren't places of labor—they were slow deaths in iron fences and blistering sun. The mechs, the overseers, the endless grind of hopelessness. He didn't need Jorek to elaborate.

"They send soldiers?" Zarathyn asked, his voice low, steady.

Jorek chuckled dryly, shaking his head. "We're not important enough for a garrison. Just the Overseer. No need for an army when you've got one like him. Bastard's got a reputation. Heard he used to gut deserters just to make a point."

The way Jorek spoke of the Overseer made Zarathyn's chest tighten. The fear wasn't just in the words; it was in the pauses, the averted gaze, the quiet tension that settled in his shoulders.

"You've met him?" Zarathyn pressed.

"Don't have to," Jorek said simply. "He doesn't bother with talk. Just shows up, takes what he wants, leaves a corpse if someone so much as looks at him wrong."

Zarathyn said nothing, though his grip on the plow tightened until his knuckles cracked. The Dominion's corruption wasn't new to him, but hearing it spelled out so plainly—watching its victims scrape life from the dirt with tools better suited for scrap—stirred something ugly in his chest. He thought of the villagers, too frightened to even speak loudly in their own homes, and of the labor camps he had escaped. It was all the same machine, grinding people into nothing.

By the time the sun dipped below the horizon, Zarathyn's back burned and his hands throbbed, but he finished the field alongside Jorek. The old man patted him on the shoulder, his grin tired but genuine. "Not bad for a drifter."

Zarathyn didn't smile back. His mind was already elsewhere, turning over everything Jorek had told him. The Dominion's grip wasn't just a problem for this village. It was a sickness that needed to be purged.

And purging was something Zarathyn had once been very, very good at.

CHAPTER 7

Zarathyn's breath came in harsh pulls as he dragged the stubborn plow through the cracked field. Every step felt heavier than the last, his borrowed strength stretched thin. Jorek worked a few paces away, muttering to himself as he swung a hoe at the unforgiving earth. The sun beat down, relentless and cruel, but Zarathyn's mind was elsewhere. He kept his gaze fixed on the ground ahead, scanning the soil with a focus that bordered on obsession.

Then he saw it—a glint, faint but unmistakable, catching the light as the plow's blade snagged on something hard beneath the dirt. Zarathyn stopped dead, his heart hammering. He bent low, his fingers clawing at the dry soil until he unearthed it: a jagged shard, barely the length of his palm, glowing faintly with a light so pale it was almost a memory of brightness.

A mana crystal. Not whole, not even close—but alive.

His hands trembled as he held it. The shard was warm, its edges biting into his palm, and for a moment, Zarathyn forgot the hunger gnawing at his belly, the ache in his muscles. A hum stirred deep within him, faint but steady, like the first note of a long-forgotten melody. It wasn't much, but it was there—a thread of magic, coiling through his veins, too weak to shape but strong enough to remind him of what he had once been.

"What've you got there?" Jorek's voice broke through the haze, sharp and suspicious.

Zarathyn tightened his grip, tucking the shard into the folds of his tunic before straightening. "Just a stone," he said, his voice steady. "Nothing worth keeping."

Jorek grunted, shrugged and went back to his hoeing, as Zarathyn returned to the plow, though his mind was already racing.

That night, long after Jorek had retired to his creaking bed, Zarathyn crouched in the corner of the barn, the shard resting on the dirt in front of him. Its faint glow barely illuminated his hands as he extended them, fingers spread wide. He closed his eyes, reaching—not with his body, but with the part of him that had once commanded storms —but the shard pushed back, its power slippery, like trying to hold water in clenched fists. Still, it responded. A faint spark jumped from the shard to his palm, a flicker of light that danced for a heartbeat before vanishing into the shadows of the barn.

Zarathyn sat back on his heels, sweat running down his brow despite the cool night air. It was small, almost laughably so compared to the power he had once commanded, but it was something. He stared at the shard, its glow dim but persistent, and felt the stirrings of something he hadn't dared to feel in years: hope.

The next night, he tried again. This time, he managed a faint breeze, a whisper of air that ruffled the hay scattered around him. It left him gasping for breath, his frail body trembling with the effort, but the hum in his veins grew stronger.

By the third night, he was summoning faint bursts of light, tiny spheres that hovered in the air for moments before winking out. The effort left him drained, his limbs weak and his head pounding, but Zarathyn gritted his teeth and kept going. Each spark, each flicker of power, brought him closer to the man he had been.

During the day, he returned to the fields, his body bent under the weight of labor but his mind racing with possibilities. He worked in silence, barely acknowledging Jorek's gruff comments or the curious stares of the other villagers. Every spare moment, every shred of energy, he poured into the shard, coaxing it to release more of its dormant power.

But the shard wasn't just restoring his magic. It was restoring him. Each night he spent channeling its energy, he felt his body push back against its frailty. His hands stopped shaking as much. His breath came a little easier. It wasn't a cure—he was still a shadow of his former self—but the difference was undeniable.

By the end of the week, Zarathyn was no longer a man simply surviving. He was rebuilding, piece by piece, spark by spark. The shard was no longer just a relic buried in the dirt. It was a weapon. A tool. A chance.

And he would use it.

***

Zarathyn's hands, once trembling like brittle leaves in the wind, now moved with a quiet steadiness. The shard hidden in his tunic burned faintly against his chest, a constant, comforting presence. His gait, once weighed down by exhaustion, carried a hint of purpose now. Not strength—not yet—but something close. Resolve, maybe. The kind that digs its heels in when the world's set against you.

By day, he worked alongside Jorek, the plow digging into the stubborn dirt. The fields were still barren, the ground cracked and defiant, but Zarathyn didn't falter. Each time the blade snagged on a hidden stone or root, his fingers itched with the urge to use the shard's power. He restrained himself, at least while the sun hung in the sky. The villagers didn't need more reasons to look at him sideways.

By night, though, his restraint faded. Zarathyn's magic came in flickers and bursts, cautious at first. In the dim light of the barn, he tested the shard's limits. He'd press his palm against a splintered axe handle, and the wood would knit itself together with a faint crackle, the jagged edges smoothing as if years of wear had been undone in seconds. The first time it worked, he felt something stir deep inside—a flicker of the man he used to be.

When he wasn't mending tools, Zarathyn turned his attention to the people. Jorek had mentioned a child, pale and fevered, barely clinging to life in the corner of a hovel that smelled of death. The mother, desperate, had tried every herb she could scavenge, but nothing stuck. Zarathyn didn't ask permission; he didn't need it. Under the cover of darkness, he slipped into the hut, his breath shallow against the sour stink of sickness.

The child was small, too small, her skin stretched tight over sharp bones. She wheezed with each breath, her chest rattling like dry leaves caught in a gust. Zarathyn knelt beside her and pressed the shard to her forehead. Its faint glow spilled over her face, illuminating every hollow and crevice. For a moment, nothing happened. Then the shard pulsed, once, and Zarathyn felt a thin thread of mana course through his veins and into the girl.

Her breathing steadied. The wheezing faded. By morning, she was sitting upright, her cheeks flushed with a hint of color. The villagers muttered about miracles, though none dared speak openly. Zarathyn stayed silent, retreating to the barn before questions could find him.

His efforts didn't go unnoticed for long. Tools that should've been useless for firewood were suddenly functional again. Crops that had been stunted for weeks showed faint signs of growth after Zarathyn spent hours near the irrigation channels, pouring mana into the cracked earth. Whispers spread, though whether they carried gratitude or suspicion depended on who you asked.

Jorek was the first to approach him directly. The old farmer cornered Zarathyn by the well one evening, his weathered face a mix of awe and caution.

"You've been busy," Jorek said, his tone low but steady.

Zarathyn met his gaze, his expression unreadable. "Someone has to be."

Jorek scratched his beard, glancing around to make sure no one was listening. "They'll notice soon. And when they do—" He paused, his voice trailing off like a man afraid to finish a sentence.

"I know," Zarathyn interrupted. His voice carried a weight that silenced any further protest. "Let them notice."

But not everyone was so willing to keep quiet. Bran, a wiry man with sharp eyes and a permanent scowl, watched Zarathyn with growing suspicion. He'd seen too much over the years—too many promises that turned to ash, too many saviors that left them worse off than before. Bran didn't trust

Zarathyn, not his quiet strength, not his sudden usefulness.

When Bran caught sight of Zarathyn slipping into the woods one night, he followed, staying far enough back to avoid detection. He didn't see much—just a faint glow spilling from the barn and the shadow of Zarathyn hunched over something —but it was enough to deepen his unease.

By the time Zarathyn returned to the barn, the mana shard thrumming faintly against his chest, he could feel the shift in the air. The villagers might not have spoken openly yet, but their whispers carried weight. Some voices held quiet hope. Others, like Bran's, carried the promise of trouble.

CHAPTER 8

Bran leaned against the fencepost, chewing on a stalk of dry grass, his sharp eyes narrowing as he watched Zarathyn's steady figure move across the fields. Something about the stranger didn't sit right with him. The man's arrival had brought change, sure, but Bran had seen change before, and it rarely came without a price.

Tools that should've stayed broken, children that should've stayed sick—these weren't miracles. They were warnings, bright flashes before the storm hit. He'd lived through too many winters, buried too many friends, to believe in good fortune without suspicion.

Jorek's voice caught Bran's ear. The old farmer was speaking to another villager, his tone low and conspiratorial.

"Don't worry about it," Jorek muttered, gesturing vaguely toward Zarathyn's silhouette in the distance. "He's helping, that's all. Everything'll be fine."

"Fine," Bran muttered under his breath, spitting the grass stalk into the dirt. He didn't trust fine. Fine was a lie you told to soothe the stupid.

Fine got people killed.

That evening, Bran sat outside his hovel, sharpening the blade of his rusted sickle. The sun dipped low, painting the sky in streaks of orange and red, but his gaze wasn't on the horizon. It was fixed on the barn, where Zarathyn had been slipping off to every night. Bran had seen the faint glow spilling from its cracks. Not the warm light of a fire—this was something colder, sharper, unnatural. He wasn't about to ignore it.

As the last rays of sunlight bled away, Zarathyn moved. Quiet as a shadow, he slipped out of Jorek's house and made his way toward the woods. Bran watched him go, the sickle resting against his knee, and then rose to his feet.

He didn't follow immediately. No, Bran was smarter than that. He waited, giving Zarathyn enough time to think he was alone. Then he moved, his steps deliberate but light, his wiry frame blending into the dusk.

The woods were dark, their twisted branches clawing at the sky, but Bran knew these paths better than most. He'd hunted here as a boy, back when the earth still gave something worth taking. His boots barely made a sound as he trailed Zarathyn, keeping his distance but never letting him out of sight.

It didn't take long to spot the stranger. Zarathyn was crouched near a clearing, his back to Bran. The faint glow returned, spilling out from between Zarathyn's fingers like liquid light. Bran couldn't see what he was holding, but the sight of it made his gut tighten.

The glow faded as quickly as it had come, and Zarathyn stood, glancing around. Bran pressed himself against a tree, holding his breath as the stranger scanned the woods. When Zarathyn finally turned and made his way back toward the barn, Bran followed, his steps slower now, more cautious.

By the time Bran reached the edge of the village, Zarathyn was already inside the barn. Bran crouched behind a pile of firewood, watching the cracks in the barn's walls. The glow returned, brighter this time, leaking out in jagged lines. Bran's heart hammered against his ribs.

"Magic," he hissed under his breath. He spat into the dirt, his lip curling. Magic had no place here. It was a tool of the Dominion, a leash used to drag men to their deaths. Whatever Zarathyn was doing, it wasn't to help them. No, this stranger was trouble, the kind that came with blood and fire and ruin.

Bran gripped the handle of his sickle, his knuckles turning white. He'd seen enough. Tomorrow, he'd speak to the others. Secrets like this didn't stay buried for long, and if Zarathyn thought he could worm his way into their village with his glowing tricks, he was about to learn how wrong he was.

The next morning

The sun crept sluggishly over the jagged

treeline, its feeble light cutting through the gray haze that seemed to hang over the village like a curse. At the well, the air was heavy with more than just the weight of another thankless day. Bran was there, leaning against the stone rim, his wiry frame taut as a bowstring. His voice, sharp and loud, rang out like the crack of an axe against brittle wood.

"Strangers," he muttered, just loud enough to turn heads. "Always the same, ain't they? They show up, do a little good, and then we pay the price. Burned crops. Dead kin. Dominion boots stomping through the fields. It's always the same."

The murmur of morning conversation faltered. Villagers paused mid-step, buckets in hand, their tired eyes darting between Bran and Zarathyn, who stood a short distance away, his back straight and his expression blank.

Bran's lips twisted into a sneer. "And here we are, taking him in like fools. Like we ain't got enough trouble already." He spat into the dirt for good measure, the gesture more venom than necessity.

A few villagers muttered in agreement, their words low but charged with unease. A woman clutching a sickly child to her chest whispered, "What if he brings them here? The Overseer won't need much of an excuse."

"But what's he done wrong?" snapped another, an older man whose face was lined like a dried riverbed. "Jorek says he's been helping. Fixed my axe, didn't he? And the boy, Ralen—he's been up and running since last night. No fever, no coughing."

Bran rounded on the man, his eyes narrowing. "Fixed tools and a fever, you think that's worth risking your neck? Risking all our necks? Don't be thick."

The murmurs grew louder, a ripple of argument spreading through the gathered crowd. Some nodded along with Bran, their faces etched with fear and doubt, while others looked at Zarathyn, standing silent and unmoving, like they wanted to speak but couldn't find the words.

Jorek pushed his way through the throng, his broad shoulders parting the villagers like a plow through dirt. "Enough!" he barked, his voice rough but firm. He planted himself between Bran and Zarathyn, his calloused hands resting on his hips. "This ain't the time for this nonsense. We've got work to do."

Bran didn't back down. "Work ain't gonna matter if the Dominion comes knocking, Jorek. You know it. We've seen it before. They'll take what they want and leave us with ashes."

"And what would you have us do?" Jorek snapped, his voice rising. "Throw him out? Leave him to starve or worse? That's not who we are."

Bran jabbed a finger toward Zarathyn, his voice dripping with accusation. "He ain't one of us. That's the point."

The crowd wavered, their gazes shifting

between Jorek and Bran. Zarathyn, still silent, met Bran's glare with a cold, unflinching stare. The tension was a living thing, pressing down on them, thick and suffocating.

A young girl clutched her mother's skirt, her voice small and trembling. "But he helped Papa..."

Bran's face twisted, his anger flickering for a moment into something almost like shame. Almost. He shook his head, his voice quieter but no less venomous. "Helped, sure. But at what cost?"

The villagers fell silent, their fear and exhaustion written plainly on their faces. They were caught in the web of their own doubts, pulled between gratitude and dread.

Jorek, his jaw tight, turned to Zarathyn. "You've done good here," he said, loud enough for everyone to hear. "We see it. But folks are scared, and scared folk make bad choices. Maybe... maybe it's best you keep your head down for now. Let things cool off."

Zarathyn's expression didn't change, but his eyes, sharp and piercing, flicked to Jorek. He gave a single, measured nod before turning on his heel and walking away, his steps steady, deliberate.

As the crowd began to disperse, Bran stayed by the well, his gaze locked on Zarathyn's retreating back. His knuckles whitened against the handle of his sickle, and his voice carried softly, almost to himself, but loud enough to stick in the air like a thorn.

"He's hiding something," he muttered. "And I'll

find out what."

***

The sun hung low, bleeding orange and crimson across the horizon as Zarathyn worked in the shadow of the barn. The plow blade lay before him, split clean down the middle, a victim of rust and years of overuse. He knelt, his fingers trembling slightly as he guided the faint shimmer of mana from the shard tucked in his palm. The magic hissed softly, like embers catching flame, as it seeped into the metal, pulling the jagged edges together inch by inch. Sweat rolled down his brow, but he didn't wipe it away. He couldn't afford distractions.

The trickle of power wasn't much—barely a whisper of what he once commanded—but it was enough to knit the steel back together. His breath steadied, and he almost allowed himself to feel a sliver of pride. Almost.

A sharp intake of breath behind him froze Zarathyn in place. His eyes snapped up from the blade, his senses suddenly alive. Slowly, he turned his head, the faint glow of magic still lingering in his hands.

Bran stood in the doorway, his face twisted in a mix of triumph and fear. His knuckles were bone-white as he gripped the handle of his sickle. "I knew it," Bran hissed, his voice a venomous whisper. "You're a damned witch."

Zarathyn straightened slowly, letting the plow

blade rest on the ground. His mind raced, every possible excuse or explanation tumbling over itself before crumbling to dust. The look in Bran's eyes told him there was no use. Denials wouldn't matter.

Bran took a step forward, his sickle raised like he might strike. "You think you can fool us? Help a few sick kids, fix a few tools, and we won't notice what you are?" His voice rose, sharp and jagged. "It's people like you that bring the Dominion down on villages like ours!"

Zarathyn's gaze hardened, the icy calm of years of survival settling over him like a shroud. He took a single step forward, closing the distance between them. Bran flinched but held his ground.

"Yes," Zarathyn said, his voice low and even. "I can use magic." He let the words hang in the air, heavy and undeniable. "But if I wanted to harm this village, you'd already know it."

Bran's lips curled, but he didn't interrupt. Zarathyn pressed on, his tone cutting like a blade. "Do you think the Overseer doesn't know you're here? He knows. He doesn't care because you're nothing to him. Just another village to bleed dry. If he thought for a moment there was magic here, he wouldn't send soldiers. He'd send fire."

Bran's grip on the sickle tightened, his knuckles trembling. "And what stops him now, huh? You? You think you're some kind of savior?"

"No," Zarathyn replied, his voice like frost. "I think I'm a man trying to help. Quietly. Carefully.

CRAIG ZERF

And I think shouting 'witch' at the top of your lungs is the quickest way to get everyone you care about killed."

Bran's face twisted, his anger and suspicion warring with the truth of Zarathyn's words. For a long moment, they stood there, locked in a silent battle of wills. Then, without another word, Bran turned on his heel and stormed out of the barn, his footsteps heavy against the packed dirt.

Zarathyn's shoulders sagged as soon as Bran was gone. The glow of the shard dimmed in his hand, the magic fading as he shoved it deep into his pocket. He stared down at the mended plow blade, the faintest of cracks still visible along the seam. A bitter smile tugged at his lips. It wasn't perfect, but it would hold.

The rumors started the next day.

It began as whispers—Bran's voice, low and urgent, carried from one villager to the next. "He's hiding something," he said. "I saw it with my own eyes. Magic. Witchcraft." The words took root in the fertile soil of fear and weariness, spreading like weeds.

By midday, the villagers' glances were no longer fleeting. Conversations stopped when Zarathyn passed by. Children were pulled closer to their parents. Even Jorek, sturdy and kind-hearted as ever, seemed quieter than usual.

Zarathyn felt the weight of it pressing down on him, a gnawing unease that clung to his every step. He considered leaving—packing up what little he had and disappearing into the woods before the tension snapped into violence. It would be easy. Safer.

But as the thought crossed his mind, he saw the boy, Ralen, running through the fields, his laugh bright and careless. The same boy who'd been too weak to sit upright just days before. He saw the old man chopping wood with the axe Zarathyn had repaired, the blade biting clean and true with every swing.

He couldn't leave. Not yet.

For the first time in years, Zarathyn felt something stir within him—something fragile but insistent. Purpose.

The villagers might fear him now, but fear could be weathered. Trust could be earned.

CHAPTER 9

The tension in the village felt like a storm gathering on the horizon. Conversations quieted as Zarathyn passed, eyes sliding away like skittish animals. The well, once a hub of tired smiles and fleeting jokes, had become a place of furtive whispers and pointed glances. Zarathyn bore it in silence, his strides deliberate, his face betraying nothing. But inside, doubt gnawed at him.

It was Bran who started it, of course. He stood at the well, his voice loud enough to carry across the market square.

"You've all heard of Ryvath, haven't you?" Bran's wiry frame seemed taller, his sharp features etched with smug confidence. "The Overseer doesn't need much of a reason to come calling. You think he won't notice magic creeping out of some backwater like ours?" He let the question hang, his eyes darting to Zarathyn like a hawk sizing up prey. "It's not just us he'll punish. He'll torch the fields, string us up to make an example. All because of him."

The name Ryvath landed like a stone dropped in a still pond. Mothers clutched their children.

The old men exchanged grim looks, their faces tight with unspoken memories. Zarathyn didn't flinch, though the weight of every gaze pressing against him felt like an anvil.

The Overseer's reputation was well-earned. Ryvath wasn't just cruel—he was systematic, efficient. A raid meant scorched earth and blood-soaked dirt. Survivors, if there were any, spoke of villages left gutted, bodies hanging from roadside gibbets to serve as grim warnings.

Zarathyn said nothing, his face blank, but Bran saw the silence as weakness. He pressed on.

"We've scraped by because we've kept our heads down. We don't need strangers bringing trouble!" He jabbed a finger toward Zarathyn, his voice rising. "You think Ryvath cares if this one's been helpful? He'll burn the lot of us just to make a point!"

The crowd murmured uneasily. Some nodded, fear plain on their faces. Others hesitated, glancing at Zarathyn with uncertainty.

It was Jorek who finally stepped forward.

The farmer was built like the land he worked— broad, steady, and worn by years of backbreaking labor. His voice carried none of Bran's sharpness, but it struck harder for its quiet strength.

"That's enough," Jorek said, his tone like the first rumble of distant thunder. He stood beside Zarathyn, planting himself between the stranger and the rest of the villagers. "You talk big about keeping the village safe, but all I hear is fear doing your thinking for you."

Bran opened his mouth to argue, but Jorek cut him off with a hard look.

"This man's done nothing but help since he got here. Fixed tools. Helped the sick. You want to turn him out because you're scared? Fine. But don't pretend it's for our sake."

For a moment, the crowd stilled. Bran scowled but said nothing. Yet even as Jorek spoke, Zarathyn's thoughts churned.

He didn't miss the way some villagers still shifted uneasily, their eyes filled with doubt. Jorek's words might have stopped the worst of the grumbling, but they hadn't erased the fear Bran had stirred. And fear had a way of festering.

That night, Zarathyn sat alone in the barn, his back against the rough planks. The shard of mana rested in his palm, its faint glow pulsing like a dying heartbeat. His fingers curled around it as he stared into the darkness, thoughts running in circles.

Ryvath was no idle threat. Zarathyn knew the Overseer's kind all too well—merciless, methodical, and utterly unconcerned with justice. If Ryvath learned of his presence here, the village wouldn't stand a chance. And Zarathyn? He was nowhere near powerful enough to challenge someone like that. Not yet.

He looked down at the shard, its glow barely illuminating his scarred hand. The magic was coming back to him, yes. But slowly. Every spell drained him more than it should, left him weaker than he could afford to be. He wasn't ready, not for Ryvath, not for anyone of his ilk.

If he stayed, he would only put the villagers in more danger. Bran's words, spiteful as they were, held a kernel of truth. Zarathyn clenched his fist around the shard, its edges biting into his palm.

He didn't want to leave. For the first time in years, he'd felt a flicker of purpose, a chance to do something good. But staying meant risking everything—and not just for himself. Jorek, the villagers, even the children he'd helped in secret... they'd all pay the price if Ryvath came.

The shard pulsed once more, a weak, steady glow. Zarathyn closed his eyes, his jaw tightening.

Leaving would be the smart choice. The right choice. But knowing that didn't make it any easier.

***

The decision, in Bran's mind, was as simple as it was cowardly. The Dominium had kept its boot on the village's neck for years, and Bran figured if someone was going to be crushed under it, better the outsider than him. He spent a restless night scribbling the letter, hunched over a battered table in his hut. The quill scratched against the parchment like a blade on bone. His hands trembled—not with guilt, but with anticipation.

"To the esteemed officials of the Dominion," he began, the words dripping with false deference. He described Zarathyn as a shadowy fugitive, dangerous and unpredictable, cloaked in magic that could bring ruin to all. Bran spun his tale with the careful malice of a snake coiling to strike. He ended with a plea for immediate intervention, signing his name with a flourish that reeked of self-righteousness.

By dawn, the letter was sealed and in the hands of a merchant heading toward the Dominion outpost. Bran watched the cart trundle away, his sharp features twisted into a grin that didn't reach his eyes. He imagined the Overseer reading his words, the grim satisfaction of knowing he'd saved his own skin—and maybe earned himself some favor in the process.

But Bran was a fool.

The Overseer, Ryvath, didn't waste time with formalities. The report reached his desk in the middle of a cold, gray afternoon, and his reaction was as swift as it was brutal. A village harboring a mage? Potential defiance of Dominion law? That wasn't just a threat to be quashed—it was an excuse to remind the region who held the leash.

He stood, the mana crystal embedded in his office wall casting a faint, eerie glow across his scarred face. Without a word, he strode toward the massive steel frame that loomed at the edge of the room—a hulking mana-powered mech suit that hissed and clicked as he approached. Its surface gleamed, a patchwork of reinforced plating engraved with Dominion insignias. The core of the suit pulsed with a dull blue light, an unmistakable reminder of the magic fueling its every move.

With practiced precision, Ryvath stepped into the suit, the mechanisms whirring as the cockpit closed around him. The mana core flared briefly, sending a ripple of energy through the air. He flexed the suit's mechanical arms, each motion accompanied by a low, guttural hum. The Overseer didn't just lead his enforcers—he towered over them, a walking reminder of the Dominion's power.

"Mount up," he barked, his voice now amplified by the mech's speaker, resonating with a metallic growl. His enforcers scrambled to obey, their horses stamping and snorting as they prepared for the march. They were more beasts than men, a mix of mercenaries and deserters held together by greed and Ryvath's iron will. Ryvath didn't ask for loyalty. He demanded fear.

The mech suit's legs groaned as it took its first steps, the ground shuddering slightly under its weight. Behind him, his riders fell into formation, their armor catching the last light of the day. "We ride at dawn," Ryvath growled, his tone cold and unrelenting. "I want the village surrounded before they even know we're there."

CHAPTER 10

The decision, in Bran's mind, was as simple as it was cowardly. The Dominium had kept its boot on the village's neck for years, and Bran figured if someone was going to be crushed under it, better the outsider than him. He spent a restless night scribbling the letter, hunched over a battered table in his hut. The quill scratched against the parchment like a blade on bone. His hands trembled—not with guilt, but with anticipation.

"To the esteemed officials of the Dominion," he began, the words dripping with false deference. He described Zarathyn as a shadowy fugitive, dangerous and unpredictable, cloaked in magic that could bring ruin to all. Bran spun his tale with the careful malice of a snake coiling to strike. He ended with a plea for immediate intervention, signing his name with a flourish that reeked of self-righteousness.

By dawn, the letter was sealed and in the hands of a merchant heading toward the Dominion outpost. Bran watched the cart trundle away, his sharp features twisted into a grin that didn't reach his eyes. He imagined the Overseer reading his words, the grim satisfaction of knowing he'd saved his own skin—and maybe earned himself some favor in the process.

But Bran was a fool.

The Overseer, Ryvath, didn't waste time with formalities. The report reached his desk in the middle of a cold, gray afternoon, and his reaction was as swift as it was brutal. A village harboring a mage? Potential defiance of Dominion law? That wasn't just a threat to be quashed—it was an excuse to remind the region who held the leash.

He stood, the mana crystal embedded in his office wall casting a faint, eerie glow across his scarred face. Without a word, he strode toward the massive steel frame that loomed at the edge of the room—a hulking mana-powered mech suit that hissed and clicked as he approached. Its surface gleamed, a patchwork of reinforced plating engraved with Dominion insignias. The core of the suit pulsed with a dull blue light, an unmistakable reminder of the magic fueling its every move.

With practiced precision, Ryvath stepped into the suit, the mechanisms whirring as the cockpit closed around him. The mana core flared briefly, sending a ripple of energy through the air. He flexed the suit's mechanical arms, each motion accompanied by a low, guttural hum. The Overseer didn't just lead his enforcers—he towered over them, a walking reminder of the Dominion's power.

"Mount up," he barked, his voice now amplified

by the mech's speaker, resonating with a metallic growl. His enforcers scrambled to obey, their horses stamping and snorting as they prepared for the march. They were more beasts than men, a mix of mercenaries and deserters held together by greed and Ryvath's iron will. Ryvath didn't ask for loyalty. He demanded fear.

The mech suit's legs groaned as it took its first steps, the ground shuddering slightly under its weight. Behind him, his riders fell into formation, their armor catching the last light of the day. "We ride at dusk," Ryvath growled, his tone cold and unrelenting. "I want the village surrounded before they even know we're there."

Unaware of the storm Bran had unleashed, the villagers went about their evening routines with a tension that had become all too familiar. Jorek, as always, worked until his hands were raw, tending to the fields as the sun sank behind the hills. Children played in the fading light, their laughter thin and brittle.

And Zarathyn?

Zarathyn was already gone.

He'd slipped away in the dead of night, his footsteps silent on the dirt path leading out of the village. The barn where he had spent so many restless nights was empty, save for a few scattered tools and a faint shimmer of mana residue that clung to the air like a ghost.

Jorek was the first to notice his absence. He'd gone to the barn at dawn, intending to bring

Zarathyn some bread and dried meat, only to find the place cold and still. He stood there for a long moment, the realization sinking in like a weight on his chest.

"He knew," Jorek muttered under his breath. "He knew this place couldn't hold him."

Back in the village, Bran strutted about, oblivious to Zarathyn's departure. He assumed his plan was unfolding perfectly, that soon the Overseer would sweep in and rid the village of its problem. He didn't consider, even for a moment, that Zarathyn might have anticipated his betrayal.

But Zarathyn had known.

The whispers, the sideways glances, Bran's pointed accusations—it had all been building to something. And though Zarathyn had felt the pull to stay, to protect these people who barely tolerated him, he'd seen the writing on the wall. If he stayed, he'd bring ruin to their doors.

So, he left.

As the sun rose above the horizon, Ryvath and his men rode out, the mech suit a hulking silhouette against the dying light. Horses' hooves pounded like war drums, a cacophony that seemed to shake the air itself. They moved with practiced efficiency, a pack of wolves closing in on unsuspecting prey.

By the time they reached the village, there would be nothing left of Zarathyn but the faintest echo of his magic, a trace too weak to satisfy the Overseer's thirst for blood. And when Ryvath found Bran, his cowardice laid bare under the Dominion's cold scrutiny, the traitor would realize too late that he had only traded one danger for another.

***

The ground quaked under the weight of Ryvath's mana-powered mech suit as he marched into the village, flanked by his enforcers. The horses of his men snorted and stamped, their riders clad in patchwork armor smeared with rust and blood. The village seemed to shrink under their approach, the houses huddling together like frightened children. Smoke from chimneys curled weakly in the cold air, the scent of burnt wood mingling with the metallic tang of the mech suit's mana core, which thrummed with each calculated step.

Ryvath's amplified voice shattered the uneasy silence. "Bring me Bran!"

The villagers hesitated, glancing at one another with the hollow-eyed fear of rabbits in a trap. A moment passed, then another, until Bran emerged from his hovel, his face a mask of smug defiance thinly painted over cowardice. He dusted his hands on his worn tunic and puffed out his chest, forcing a grin as if trying to convince himself he wasn't terrified.

"Overseer Ryvath," Bran said, his voice wavering ever so slightly, "I see you've come quickly. I knew the Dominium would act swiftly against such threats."

Ryvath's helm turned slightly, the glowing slits of its visor fixing on Bran like the cold stare of death itself. "Show me," he said simply, his voice carrying the promise of violence.

Bran, eager to please, scurried toward the barn, his boots crunching on the frost-hardened ground. He glanced back over his shoulder, flashing a nervous smile. "Right this way, Overseer. You'll see I wasn't lying. He's been hiding in here."

The barn door creaked loudly as Bran pushed it open, the sound grating against the tense stillness. Dust motes swirled in the pale light spilling in from outside. The place was empty. No sign of Zarathyn. No bedroll, no supplies—nothing.

Bran froze. His heart sank, panic blooming in his chest like a spreading fire. "No, no, no," he muttered, his voice pitching higher with each word. "He was here! He was right here!"

Ryvath stepped forward, his suit's servos whining as he crouched to inspect the space. A low, distorted hum emanated from the mech as he activated a mana scanner. The faint residue confirmed that magic had been here, but it was weak, dissipating. Too old to be useful.

The Overseer rose, towering over Bran. "Where is he?" Ryvath's voice cut through the barn like a blade.

Bran stammered, his hands flailing as if grasping for an explanation. "I—I swear he was here! The villagers—ask them! They must know!"

Ryvath didn't respond. Instead, he turned sharply and marched out of the barn, his enforcers falling in behind him. The villagers had gathered now, clustered in tight knots, their faces pale and drawn. Ryvath's gaze swept over them, his visor's glow casting a sinister light.

The ground seemed to freeze harder beneath the weight of Ryvath's mech as he turned to the gathered villagers. His visor glowed with a cold, menacing light, illuminating their pale, pinched faces. His amplified voice thundered over the silence, sending shivers down spines.

"Speak," he commanded, his tone like an avalanche bearing down on them. "Who here harbored the fugitive?"

The villagers shifted uneasily, a collective murmur of boots scraping against the frozen ground. No one dared to meet Ryvath's gaze. An old woman crossed herself, lips trembling with a prayer that died as quickly as it was born.

They all knew what was at stake. Ryvath didn't deal in nuance or half-measures. If a village was found guilty of harboring a fugitive, the punishment would fall like a hammer on everyone—guilty or not. Burnt homes, slaughtered livestock, and the occasional execution of anyone deemed "complicit" were the Dominium's signature warnings. The overseer didn't need proof; suspicion alone was enough to raze everything they'd worked for into ash.

A younger man stepped forward, his hands

trembling as if the cold had finally sunk into his bones. "We don't know what you're talking about, Overseer," he said, his voice slow, careful, and laced with fear. "There's no fugitive here."

The others murmured their agreement, their voices quiet but firm. They clung to a fragile unity, an unspoken pact forming in their shared, desperate glances. Bran's betrayal had brought this storm to their doorstep, and if Ryvath needed someone to punish, then so be it—let the despicable Bran take the fall.

Bran's face twisted in shock and rage. "You're lying!" he shouted, his voice breaking with panic. He turned to Ryvath, his gestures frantic, pointing at the crowd like a cornered rat baring its teeth. "They know! They helped him! They're trying to protect him!"

Ryvath's helm turned toward Bran with a slow, deliberate precision. The ominous hum of the mana core in his mech filled the uneasy silence, punctuated only by the faint creak of leather and the nervous snorts of horses.

The Overseer advanced, each step a heavy thud that sent tremors through the earth. His steel-clad fingers extended, gripping Bran's shoulder with a force that made the traitor yelp. Bran stumbled, his knees nearly buckling under the weight of Ryvath's grip.

"You wasted my time," Ryvath said, his voice devoid of emotion but carrying the weight of a death sentence. "And theirs." He gestured vaguely toward the villagers, the implication clear.

"No, please! No!" Bran shrieked, his voice cracking as he clawed at the Overseer's arm. "I told the truth! He was here! You have to believe me!"

Ryvath didn't respond. Instead, the blade on his mech's other arm unfolded with a metallic hiss, glinting wickedly in the pale light. With a motion as swift as it was brutal, he drove the blade into Bran's abdomen, the metal slicing through flesh and muscle like butter.

Bran's scream pierced the air, high and sharp, before choking off into a wet, gurgling sound. Blood poured from the wound, steaming as it hit the frozen ground, pooling dark and thick beneath his writhing body. Ryvath twisted the blade, then yanked it free with a sickening squelch. Bran collapsed in a heap, his hands scrabbling weakly at his stomach, his eyes wide with terror and agony.

The villagers didn't move. They barely breathed. A few turned their faces away, unable to watch, while others stared, their expressions blank, as if willing themselves to feel nothing.

"String him up," Ryvath said coldly, his tone as casual as if he were discussing the weather.

Two enforcers dismounted, their boots crunching through the blood-soaked dirt. They grabbed Bran's twitching body, dragging him toward a gnarled tree that stood at the edge of the square. His feeble attempts to resist were pitiful, his limbs flopping uselessly as they hauled him into place.

A rope was thrown over a low-hanging branch. They tied it beneath Bran's arms, ignoring his weak, gasping protests as they hoisted him upright. Blood dripped steadily from his gaping wound, streaking his legs and pattering onto the ground below.

The villagers stared, their expressions frozen masks of fear and grim acceptance. They knew better than to speak, to intervene, to draw any more attention to themselves. If the Dominium demanded blood, it was better Bran's than theirs.

Ryvath turned to the villagers one last time, his voice booming as he delivered his final warning. "Let this be a reminder. Lies waste my time. And wasting my time costs lives."

Without another glance, he pivoted, his mech's servos hissing as he strode toward the edge of the village. His enforcers mounted their horses and followed, leaving behind the grotesque, swaying figure of Bran's body as a grim monument to the Dominium's wrath.

And the villagers, bound by silence and fear, simply stood there, unable to look away from the bloody reminder of how precarious their lives truly were.

CHAPTER 11

Zarathyn stumbled into the Endless Forest, his legs like lead and his breath ragged, each step dragging him deeper into the shadowed abyss. The night was thick, choked with fog and the endless chirp of insects that never seemed to stop, a low hum that gnawed at his sanity. The trees towered above him, hunched like ancient guardians, their gnarled branches twisting in shapes that seemed to reach for him, clawing at his skin. He felt the weight of their eyes—if trees had eyes.

His magic was all but spent. Every time he pushed himself to pull another spark from the depths, it felt like ripping at an empty well, hoping for just a drop. He could feel the sharp bite of exhaustion in his limbs, the dark press of hunger gnawing at his stomach. And the cold... it was brutal, sharp enough to make his bones ache. A chill that worked its way into his soul, setting his teeth on edge.

Zarathyn's coat, soaked from sweat and rain, did little to stave off the biting wind. The last remnants of his magic were sloshed together in a desperate, shaky flicker of flame. It sputtered like a dying candle, but it was enough to warm his hands for a moment—enough to keep the worst of the cold at bay. He concentrated on it, feeding the flames just enough to keep from freezing in place, but it was barely a comfort.

He pushed on, weaving through the twisted trees that leaned in as if trying to shove him off his path. Each step seemed to lead deeper into the heart of the forest, and with every crack of a branch underfoot, his paranoia flared. Someone— or something—was watching him. The sense of it was undeniable. The forest had a way of making you feel small, like prey, even when you were the one hunting. His hand itched for the dagger at his belt, but he knew it wouldn't do much good against what might be lurking in the shadows.

His stomach twisted in hunger, a gnawing, relentless ache that made his body want to betray him. But there was no time to stop. No time to be weak. He forced himself forward, keeping his senses sharp. It wasn't just the cold or hunger he had to fight—it was the realization that the patrols would be looking for him soon. If they weren't already. He could hear the distant, muffled echoes of something—some thing—moving deeper in the woods, but it was hard to tell if it was his mind playing tricks or the forest itself. The sounds here weren't like anything he'd ever known, full of strange rustlings and the occasional screech of an animal too wild to name.

A snap of a twig—a flash of movement—had

him whipping his head around, the magic inside him flaring. His hand clenched around the hilt of his dagger, and his heart hammered in his chest. He stood frozen, every muscle wound tight, every nerve alert. But the darkness didn't give up its secrets easily. Whatever it was, it stayed hidden in the dark.

A grunt of frustration left him as he finally pushed on, moving faster now, though every step felt like a drag through molasses. He wasn't sure if he was looking for safety, or if he was just running away from the terror closing in behind him. Or both. The forest felt alive in a way he wasn't used to, like it was waiting for something. Or worse —waiting for him to make a mistake. But there was no choice. Every direction led deeper into the forest. And if he didn't get a fire going soon, he'd freeze before the morning light broke through the canopy.

Finally, after what felt like hours, he spotted a pile of dry twigs and leaves, gathered together by the whim of fate or something else. He knelt down, his fingers numb as he pulled together what little he had left in him. A small spark. Another. A flicker of fire.

It came to life with a crackle, weak but enough. Zarathyn huddled close, feeding the tiny flame, coaxing it to grow. The cold didn't let up, but at least the fire offered a sliver of warmth. Just enough to remind him that he wasn't completely gone yet. That he was still alive, still fighting. The fire danced in his tired eyes, like a cruel joke. A reminder of how close he was to death. And of how close he had come to failing.

In the flickering shadows of the firelight, Zarathyn pressed a hand to his chest, feeling his heart race. The panic clawed at him again. He was alone. Alone in a forest that had never been kind to anyone. Alone in a world that wanted him dead.

His mind drifted back to the patrols. Ryvath. The enforcers. The storm of betrayal that had been waiting for him in that damnable village. The thought of Bran's face, that smug bastard, turning him over like a lamb to the slaughter, sent a wave of heat flooding his chest. A fire different from the one he had kindling before him.

But he couldn't afford to let that rage burn him. Not here. Not now. He'd need every ounce of focus to make it through this forest. His enemies were out there. And they weren't going to stop until he was dead.

Zarathyn leaned closer to the fire, forcing himself to steady his breath. The gnawing cold eased a little, but he was far from safe. He wasn't even close to knowing what awaited him next in this endless, wretched forest.

The forest came alive at night, and not in a way that offered comfort. Zarathyn crouched low behind a thicket of brambles, his fingers tightening around the dagger at his side. His breathing was shallow, and every exhale fogged the air in front of him. Somewhere out there, beyond the twisted trunks and whispering leaves, it waited. The beast. He hadn't seen it clearly—just a flash of those red eyes, burning like coals in the darkness. But the sound it made, that guttural, rumbling growl—it stuck in his chest like a spear.

The first time it came close, he'd nearly bolted. Panic surged in his veins, his body screaming at him to run. But he wasn't stupid. Running would make him prey. And this thing, whatever it was, wasn't just hunting. It was stalking. Playing. A predator that enjoyed the chase.

His mind raced as he clutched a bundle of dry kindling he'd been gathering for a fire. Fire. That was his answer. If there was one thing every predator feared, it was flame. He scrambled, fumbling with his meager reserves of magic, forcing a flicker of heat to his fingertips. It wasn't much—his mana felt like a shallow pool, nearly drained from days of survival and constant vigilance—but it would have to do.

The first spark caught, and the kindling flared to life in a bright orange burst. Zarathyn worked quickly, fanning the flames until they roared higher. Then, with a grunt, he heaved the pile toward a hollow between the trees. The firelight danced wildly, casting long, erratic shadows that flickered across the forest floor. It wasn't much, but it was enough to fool a creature relying on its sight.

He didn't wait to see if the beast fell for the trick. Scrambling to his feet, he bolted toward the nearest rocky rise, his boots slipping on the damp ground as he half-ran, half-crawled up the jagged incline. The rock tore at his hands, and his legs burned with the effort, but he didn't stop. Couldn't stop.

Below, the fire crackled louder, and he heard it—the low, menacing snarl of the beast. It was close. Too close. He flattened himself against the cold stone of the outcrop, his breath hitching as the sound of heavy paws crunched through the underbrush.

The thing stalked into view, and Zarathyn's gut twisted. It was massive, taller than any wolf he'd ever seen, with fur blacker than midnight and eyes that gleamed with an unnatural red light. Its maw was lined with teeth that seemed too large for its mouth, jagged and dripping with saliva that hissed when it hit the dirt.

It sniffed the air, then turned its head toward the decoy fire. Zarathyn's heart hammered as he watched it slink closer, its movements too smooth, too deliberate. The firelight reflected off its eyes, giving it an almost demonic glow.

Then, with a low growl, it leapt, snapping its jaws at the flames before recoiling, confused. The distraction had worked—for now. Zarathyn pressed his back harder against the rock, biting back a cry of relief.

The next day was no kinder. His stomach was a gnawing pit of emptiness, and the meager handful of dried berries he'd scrounged earlier had done little to stave off the hunger. He had to eat. His magic was too weak to keep him going for long, and without food, it would fail him entirely.

He moved cautiously, his ears straining for any sound beyond the rustling leaves and distant bird calls. The forest was full of life, but catching it was another matter.

His first attempt at hunting had been an embarrassing failure. He'd seen a rabbit darting between the roots of a fallen tree and had loosed a small firebolt in desperation. The blast had missed, scorching the earth and sending the rabbit fleeing deeper into the underbrush. The smell of burnt dirt lingered long after the humiliation had faded.

By the afternoon, he'd managed to cobble together a crude snare using strips of his fraying cloak and a bent branch. It wasn't elegant, but it worked. The bird he caught—a scraggly thing with feathers mottled gray and white—was barely enough for a mouthful, but he didn't care.

The kill was messy. He'd hesitated at first, staring at the fluttering, panicked creature as it struggled against the snare. But hunger didn't allow for kindness. His hands trembled as he broke its neck, and he muttered a quiet apology to the forest before plucking it clean.

The fire he cooked it over was small, little more than a pile of embers nestled between stones. The smell of charred meat filled the air, and Zarathyn's stomach growled so loud it startled him. He tore into the bird the moment it was cool enough to touch, ignoring the bitter, gamey taste and the way the meat stuck to his teeth.

By the third night, exhaustion had turned to fury. Bran's face haunted him in the flicker of every firelight, his smug grin twisting into a sneer that seemed to mock Zarathyn's every failure. The betrayal cut deeper than the hunger or the cold, a wound that refused to heal.

He wanted to hate Bran, and he did—but there was more. Regret gnawed at him, too. He'd left the villagers behind, left them to face the Overseer's wrath. He'd run while they stayed. Coward.

And then there was the fear, the quiet, insidious thought that whispered in the back of his mind. That he wasn't enough. That no matter how much magic he learned, no matter how strong he became, he'd never be ready. Never be able to face the Overseer, the Dominium, or anything else this cursed world threw at him.

The fire crackled at his feet, the only sound in the suffocating silence of the forest. Zarathyn stared into the flames, his fists clenched so tightly his knuckles turned white. He wasn't dead yet. That had to count for something.

CHAPTER 12

The Endless Forest had its own cruel rhythm, and Zarathyn was slowly learning to dance to its tune. His first attempts at crafting tools were clumsy, the kind of work a child might be ashamed to show off. But necessity didn't care about pride. With hands calloused from scraping bark and cutting vines, he carved a rough spear from a straight branch he'd scavenged. It wasn't much— just a pointed stick, really—but with a flicker of fire magic, he hardened the tip, blackening it into something that could pierce flesh. Or, at least, he hoped it could.

The spear wasn't the only thing he built. Using the vines that dangled like nooses from the forest canopy, he fashioned traps—basic snares that relied on tension and luck. And then there was fire. His magic, so often a bludgeon, became something sharper and more precise. He could coax a flame to life on damp wood or control its shape long enough to scorch and seal. Nights in the forest were cold and unforgiving, but the fire never let him down. It became his shield, his weapon, his companion.

But the forest didn't take kindly to intruders.

Biting insects swarmed his exposed skin, leaving welts that itched and burned no matter how much he scratched. He learned quickly that scratching only made it worse, but knowing didn't stop his fingers from twitching toward the angry red bumps. His patience thinned with every buzz in his ear, every sting on his neck.

Then came the snakes. One coiled itself around a branch above his head, its scales a mosaic of green and black. He spotted it just before it struck, its fangs sinking into the air where his face had been a moment earlier. He fell backward, his spear forgotten as panic surged. The snake dropped to the ground, its body moving with an almost liquid grace as it slithered toward him. Zarathyn reacted on instinct, his hand flaring with heat as he hurled a small, concentrated firebolt. It struck true, charring the snake's head and leaving its body to twitch lifelessly on the dirt.

The cold nights were a different kind of fight. His fire magic could stave off the worst of it, but it wasn't enough to warm the ground beneath him or keep the frost from nipping at his toes. He spent hours shivering, his teeth chattering loud enough to drown out the forest's eerie whispers. Sleep came in fits, and when it did, it brought no peace.

One evening, as he scavenged for more firewood, the forest threw something new at him —a creature straight out of a nightmare. It scuttled into view on too many legs, its spindly body covered in chitinous plates that gleamed faintly under the pale light filtering through the canopy. Its head was a grotesque mash of mandibles and black, faceted eyes that reflected every flicker of his fire. It was insect-like, but far too large and far too intelligent to be mistaken for anything mundane.

Zarathyn froze, his fingers tightening around his spear. The thing hissed—a wet, rasping sound that raised every hair on his body. It lunged, and he barely managed to dodge, the creature's sharp legs gouging deep grooves in the dirt where he'd stood. His first instinct was to attack, but the spear barely scratched the surface of the beast's armored hide. It clicked its mandibles in what almost seemed like amusement before lunging again.

He ran. Not out of fear, though it coiled in his gut like a snake, but because he needed a plan. The forest's twisted terrain, its uneven roots and thick undergrowth, worked against him as much as it did the monster. His lungs burned, and his legs ached as he pushed himself harder, his mind racing for solutions.

Then he saw it—a narrow ravine, its sides lined with jagged rocks and thorny bushes. He skidded to a stop and turned, the creature closing the gap with terrifying speed. Summoning what little magic he had left, he lit a small fire in the undergrowth near the ravine's edge. The flames leaped hungrily, and the beast hesitated, its head tilting as if weighing its options. Zarathyn took the chance to circle around, taunting it with shouts and throwing small embers to steer it toward the flames.

When it finally charged, it was too late. The creature barreled straight into the fire, its legs catching in the thick, thorny bushes. It screamed —an ear-splitting, almost human wail—as the flames consumed it. Zarathyn didn't look away, even as the stench of burning chitin filled the air and the beast's thrashing grew weaker. This was survival, and survival didn't allow for hesitation or pity.

When it was over, he sank to the ground, his body trembling from more than exhaustion. The ravine still smoldered, the last remnants of the creature's body crackling softly in the dying firelight. He'd won, but the victory felt hollow.

Sleep didn't bring rest that night. When he finally drifted off, it was to a torrent of dreams that clawed at his mind. Bran's sneer loomed large, twisting into a grotesque mask that laughed at him from the shadows. The villagers were there too, their faces gaunt and accusing, their voices whispering words he couldn't understand.

And then there was the beast. Not the one he'd killed, but something larger, darker. Its red eyes burned through the dreamscape, and its growl shook the ground beneath his feet. Zarathyn woke with a start, sweat clinging to his skin despite the cold. The fire had gone out, leaving him alone in the oppressive silence of the forest.

He stared into the darkness, his hand gripping his spear tightly. The forest wasn't just testing him. It was breaking him down, piece by piece. But Zarathyn clenched his jaw and set his gaze forward. He wouldn't break. Not yet.

***

Zarathyn stumbled to the top of a ridge, his legs trembling beneath him. His breath came in short, ragged bursts, and his vision blurred from exhaustion. But when he reached the crest and looked out, he stopped cold. There it was, rising from the tangled chaos of the Endless Forest like a jagged wound against the sky—a castle.

It wasn't the kind of regal fortress told in bedtime stories. No gleaming towers or fluttering banners here. This was something older, darker. Its crumbling walls leaned precariously, draped in thick curtains of moss that spilled down like blood from an open wound. Vines gripped the stone like skeletal fingers, clawing their way up to the shattered battlements. The main tower, blackened with age, jutted into the sky like the snapped spine of some forgotten beast.

The castle's gates hung open, one tilted off its rusted hinges, the other splintered at the edges where the forest had shoved its way in. Zarathyn didn't trust the sight, but his body moved on instinct, dragging him closer. Each step down the hill felt heavier, the weight of his exhaustion pressing on his shoulders, but he couldn't turn away.

When he reached the base, the sheer size of the place struck him. Up close, the outer walls were riddled with gaps where the stones had collapsed, leaving gaping holes large enough for a wolf to squeeze through. Patches of wildflowers sprouted defiantly between the cracks, their colors muted in the shadow of the castle.

He paused at the gate, one hand brushing against the cold, rusted metal. The air here felt different. Heavy. Tainted. There was a faint thrum just beneath the surface, like a heartbeat too weak to fully sound. Magic. Old, residual, but still alive in some strange, stubborn way. It prickled at the edge of his senses, teasing him with the promise of something just out of reach.

The courtyard beyond was a battlefield between stone and nature. Trees had taken root where soldiers might once have marched, their trunks thick and gnarled, their branches twisting like desperate hands reaching for the sky. Roots had punched through the cobblestones, splitting them apart and leaving jagged edges that could slice through flesh. In the far corner, a stagnant pool of water gleamed in the weak sunlight, its surface marred by drifting leaves and the faint shimmer of something unnatural beneath.

Above, bats stirred in the hollowed-out remains of the towers, their wings rasping faintly against the stone. One screeched, breaking the oppressive silence, and Zarathyn flinched, his hand darting to the hilt of his dagger. The sound echoed, carrying through the empty halls and shadowy recesses of the castle, as if mocking his unease.

He stepped forward, his boots crunching against the loose gravel and broken stone. The scent of rot hung faintly in the air—earthy and wet, like something left to fester far too long. The walls loomed on either side, closing in, as if the castle itself was watching him.

The urge to turn back gnawed at him, a whisper of self-preservation. He was too tired, too worn to fight whatever might lurk here. But that faint pulse of magic kept pulling at him, like a thread he couldn't help but follow. His curiosity overrode his caution, and he pressed deeper into the ruins.

Every step inside felt like trespassing on sacred ground, or perhaps a graveyard. Something had happened here—something ancient and violent. He could feel it in the air, in the way the stones seemed to hum faintly beneath his feet. Whatever power had once ruled this place, it had long since been broken, but the remnants of it clung stubbornly to life, waiting for someone foolish enough to awaken it.

Zarathyn clenched his jaw and tightened his grip on his dagger. Foolish or not, he was here. And he wasn't leaving until he found out what this place had to offer.

CHAPTER 13

The moment Zarathyn stepped deeper into the castle's bowels, the air seemed to shift. It grew colder, biting at his exposed skin despite the faint glow of his fire magic flickering in his palm. His breath fogged in the dim light, swirling in ghostly patterns before vanishing into the shadows. The walls pressed in, closer and more oppressive with each step. Their stone surface, slick with moss and damp, seemed to hum faintly under his touch, as though the structure itself remembered things it wasn't eager to share.

He moved cautiously, his footsteps soft but deliberate on the uneven floor. Every sound echoed—each scrape of his boot, the faint hiss of his breath, the occasional drip of water from the ceiling above. He gritted his teeth, half-expecting a trapdoor to spring open beneath him or a rusted blade to lunge from a hidden crevice. Places like this, relics of forgotten eras, were rarely kind to trespassers.

As he rounded a corner, the faintest traces of artistry caught his eye. He brought the fire closer, and there they were—murals. Faded and fragmented, but still defiant against time. They sprawled across the walls in jagged patches, depicting scenes of mages clad in flowing robes, their hands raised in intricate gestures as they commanded storms, flames, and shimmering bolts of power. The faces were worn, their features smoothed by centuries of neglect, but the imagery was unmistakable. Zarathyn felt a chill that had nothing to do with the cold. These were the same figures he'd seen in a crumbling tome as a child, back when magic was still more fantasy than reality to him.

The Order of the Arcanum.

He didn't need the inscriptions—most of which had eroded into indecipherable lines—to recognize their iconography. A serpent devouring its tail. The spire-like towers. The seven-pointed star etched into the mages' chests. It all matched the legends he'd thought were just that: stories. Yet here he stood, surrounded by their remnants.

The murals weren't the only markers of their presence. Statues lined a crumbling corridor further in, though most had fallen. A few still stood defiantly, half-buried in rubble or leaning at precarious angles. Their faces were worn smooth, their forms cracked and eroded, but the craftsmanship—now dulled—spoke of an artistry long lost to the world. One statue caught his eye, a mage holding aloft a staff crowned with a seven-pointed star. His expression, frozen in stone, radiated defiance even as time gnawed at his features.

Zarathyn tore his gaze from the statues and pressed on, his curiosity overriding his caution. The castle seemed to pull him deeper, as if it knew he'd come searching for answers—or for power. The faint hum of magic grew stronger, more insistent, the deeper he ventured. The temperature dropped further, and his fire flared erratically, as if struggling to survive the oppressive cold.

When he pushed open a warped wooden door, the smell of rot and ancient parchment hit him like a wave. A library. Or what was left of it. Shelves loomed like skeletons, their wood cracked and bowed under the weight of ages. Many had collapsed entirely, spilling their contents into haphazard piles of decayed scrolls and brittle tomes. Zarathyn's firelight swept across the room, revealing a chaos of words—ink smeared and faded, pages curled and blackened with mildew.

Still, he pressed forward, picking through the ruins with careful hands. His heart leapt when his fingers brushed against something intact. A fragment of a scroll, its edges singed but its runes still legible. He knelt, cradling it as if it might crumble under his touch. The symbols weren't just decorative—they radiated faint magic, old but not dead. The text described basic rune crafting, the delicate art of embedding magic into physical forms. Simple stuff, perhaps, but invaluable to someone like him, clawing his way back to power.

He stuffed the fragment into his satchel and kept searching. Another scroll, this one detailing elemental affinities. A torn page from what appeared to be a journal, its writing frenzied, warning of experiments gone wrong. It was messy work—his hands blackened with soot and ink, his nails cracked from prying open crumbling covers. But it was worth it. Each scrap of knowledge was a lifeline, a step closer to becoming something more than the hunted man he was.

The library yielded little else. Most of the texts were beyond saving, their magic drained or their pages reduced to dust. But Zarathyn couldn't shake the feeling that even the fragments he'd found were meant to be his, waiting in this forgotten crypt for someone desperate—or foolish—enough to claim them.

The cold gnawed at him as he stepped back into the corridor. The faint hum of residual magic whispered at the edge of his awareness, and he followed it. There was more here, he was sure of it. More to find. More to take.

***

The spiral staircase plunged into the earth like a wound, its stone steps slick with centuries of damp. Zarathyn tested each step before fully committing his weight, his free hand skimming the crumbling wall for balance. The air was a stagnant mix of rot and mildew, thick enough to taste. His flame hovered just ahead, casting jittery shadows that made the descent feel more claustrophobic than it already was.

The walls of the dungeon were damp, almost slimy, as though the very stone had grown sick from disuse. Rusted chains hung like forgotten skeletons, their iron links flecked with orange and black, rattling faintly when his sleeve brushed too close. Water dripped from above, pooling in shallow depressions along the uneven floor. Each drop echoed like a heartbeat, loud in the stifling silence.

Then came the skeletons. Dozens of them, slumped against the walls or lying sprawled across the floor. Some were missing limbs, their bones gnawed clean—by time or something worse. A few still wore the tattered remains of their shackles, the metal having outlasted the flesh and cloth. Zarathyn didn't flinch, but he did step lightly, his boots carefully avoiding the brittle remnants of ribs and skulls. The smell of death lingered, ancient yet potent, like a room that had never fully exhaled its misery.

The faint hum of magic crept in, a whisper against the edge of his senses. It pulled him forward, guiding him deeper into the dungeon's belly. The corridors branched, twisting in maddening patterns, but the hum grew stronger as he followed it, like a thread weaving through the darkness.

Finally, he found it—a section of wall that felt wrong. It wasn't immediately obvious, but his eyes caught the faint shimmer of runes beneath a thick coat of grime. It was hidden behind a pile of debris: broken stones, splintered beams, and the remnants of what might have once been a doorway. Zarathyn knelt and pressed his palm against the rubble. The hum surged, faint but undeniable.

Clearing the obstruction wasn't easy. His fire magic flared, melting the tougher obstacles and reducing wooden beams to smoldering ash. Sweat trickled down his face as he worked, the heat of his spell mixing with the oppressive cold of the dungeon. The rubble fought back, almost as though it didn't want to be moved, but Zarathyn's persistence won out. When the last stone rolled free, a hidden door revealed itself, its surface marked with intricate sigils that glowed faintly as though they still held a grudge against the one who carved them.

The sigils were old, predating most of the magic Zarathyn had studied. But he knew enough to read their intent: protection, warning, death. Traps layered over traps. He traced his fingers over the markings, muttering softly as he pieced them together. This wasn't brute force work; it was precision. One misstep and the door might explode—or worse, lock forever.

Minutes stretched into hours as he worked, sweat cooling on his back and his magic flickering dangerously low. He adjusted runes here, redirected energy there, his lips moving in silent incantations. Finally, with a whispered command and a pulse of magic, the sigils dimmed and the door shuddered.

It creaked open reluctantly, as though the centuries had weighed it down. The chamber beyond was pristine, untouched by the decay that plagued the rest of the dungeon. Zarathyn stepped inside, and his fire magic illuminated what could only be described as a treasure hoard for a mage.

The room was small but dense with power. Crystal-tipped staves leaned against one wall, their shafts carved with glowing runes that pulsed faintly. Rings rested in careful rows atop a velvet-lined pedestal, their gemstones shimmering with preserved enchantments. Shelves of ancient tomes lined the far wall, their spines intact and their pages warded against time's decay. Piles of mana crystals sparkled and shimmered with power. The air buzzed with restrained energy, a heady mix of possibilities.

Zarathyn approached cautiously, his eyes scanning for traps, his senses on high alert. He reached out and let his fingers graze the edge of a staff. Power surged through him like a jolt of lightning, sharp and invigorating. A grin spread across his face, the first in what felt like weeks. He wasn't just surviving anymore. He was starting to rebuild.

CHAPTER 14

The artifact room, nestled deep beneath layers of stone and shadows, became Zarathyn's sanctuary. The air here was dense with untapped energy, like the hum of a storm waiting to break. He cleared the debris first, kicking aside shattered pedestals and rotting wooden shelves. The ancient room was as neglected as the castle itself, its treasures buried under layers of grime and rubble. Dust clung to his cloak and throat as he worked, his every breath harsh and dry. He didn't stop. Not until the center of the chamber was bare stone, its surface cracked and cold, ready for his transformation.

The first step was organizing the relics. Each piece was a puzzle he itched to solve. Mana crystals, glowing faintly with trapped energy, were stacked carefully in a corner. He tested each one by gripping it tightly in his palm, drawing a fraction of its power to gauge its strength. Some flared to life, warmth coursing up his arm, while others crumbled to powder, spent long before his time. The still-usable ones were sorted by intensity, arranged in concentric circles on the floor for easy access during cultivation.

The enchanted rings came next. There were dozens, some bent out of shape, others still gleaming with faint, arcane etchings. He slid a few onto his fingers, feeling their effects ripple through him—one amplified his senses, sharpening his hearing until he could catch the faint groan of stone above; another deadened his touch, leaving his fingers numb and heavy. He stripped them off just as quickly, keeping only what wouldn't hinder his movements.

The mornings were a trial in themselves. Zarathyn stepped into the overgrown courtyard before dawn, the air damp and heavy with dew, and the world painted in pale shades of gray. His staff felt solid in his grip, its weight a comfort as he moved silently through the knee-high grass. This was routine now—part of his rhythm, as natural as breathing. If he didn't hunt, he wouldn't eat. If he didn't eat, his training would falter.

The smaller prey—rabbits, squirrels, and the occasional plump bird—were easier, though never effortless. They were quick, always on edge, every rustle of grass or snap of a twig sending them darting out of reach. Zarathyn adapted. He learned to wait, to crouch low, his body still as stone, until a rabbit dared to nibble at the scattered bait he left. Then came the strike—swift and brutal. His staff came down with a crack, and the life drained from the creature in a heartbeat.

The boar, though, was another story entirely. That morning, he'd tracked its prints—deep grooves in the mud, edges clawed by the beast's hooves—and followed the trail into the denser forest. The air grew warmer as the trees thickened, and the sounds of birds and insects seemed to muffle under the weight of his focus.

When he found it, the boar was rooting through a cluster of bushes, its tusks gleaming like dull blades in the dappled light. It was massive, its thick hide matted with mud and scars, its shoulders rolling with muscle. Zarathyn's pulse quickened. This wasn't a clean, easy kill. This was a fight.

He circled slowly, staff raised, keeping himself downwind. The beast snorted, pawing the ground, but didn't notice him until it was too late. He raised his free hand, fire sparking to life in his palm. The heat built quickly, a roiling ball of flame that he hurled at the boar's side.

The fire struck, searing flesh and filling the air with the stench of burning hair. The boar bellowed in rage and pain, wheeling around to face him. Its dark eyes glinted with fury, and it charged.

Zarathyn leapt aside, his boots skidding on the damp earth, and swung his staff. The heavy wood struck the beast's flank with a sickening crack, sending it crashing into a tree. But even as it fell, it thrashed wildly, its tusks carving deep furrows into the ground. Blood sprayed in arcs, painting the forest floor in wet streaks.

He didn't wait. While the beast struggled to rise, Zarathyn lunged, driving the blunt end of his staff into its throat. The boar choked, its legs kicking out violently, but the fight was already over. When it finally stilled, he stood over it, chest heaving, sweat dripping from his brow. The ground around them was slick with blood, dark and steaming in the cool morning air.

But hunting wasn't just about the kill. After dragging the carcass back to the castle, his work was far from done. Skinning and gutting the animal was messy, backbreaking labor, and Zarathyn's hands were often slick with gore by the time he finished. He salvaged what he could—meat for roasting, sinew for binding, bones for crafting.

Foraging was another skill he'd been forced to learn. The castle ruins and the forest's edges offered more than just meat. He scoured the underbrush for roots, berries, and mushrooms, relying on trial and error to identify what wouldn't kill him. His earlier mistakes were seared into his memory—bitter leaves that had left him retching, berries that burned his tongue like acid.

Now he was cautious. He tested everything in small doses, watching for reactions before committing to a full meal. He discovered clusters of wild onions near the broken walls of the courtyard, their sharp tang cutting through the blandness of roasted meat. In the forest, he found patches of tubers, their starchy flesh a welcome addition to his meals.

Cooking was its own kind of trial. He used his fire magic to build controlled flames, roasting meat on spits fashioned from green branches or boiling water in hollowed-out stones. He learned to experiment—seasoning his food with crushed herbs or drying strips of meat over low embers to preserve them for later.

By the end of each morning, Zarathyn's body ached, his hands were raw, and his stomach was finally full. Each meal was hard-won, every bite a reminder of the savage balance of survival. But as he sat by his makeshift fire, watching the flames dance and listening to the distant howl of some unseen beast, he felt a quiet satisfaction.

This was life now. Brutal. Unforgiving. And yet, it strengthened him with every passing day.

***

Zarathyn returned to the artifact room with his haul, the faint smell of roasted meat clinging to his cloak. He set the leftovers near the embers of the firepit he'd carved into the stone floor, letting the warmth keep the meal from spoiling. The moment his hands were free, he grabbed the staff leaning against the wall. It was six feet of smooth, dark wood, streaked with veins of faintly glowing crimson. The thing pulsed faintly, like it had a heartbeat of its own. Every time he held it, his palms tingled, as if the weapon were testing his resolve.

The staff wasn't just a tool—it was a beast to be tamed. At first, channeling magic through it had nearly flayed the skin from his hands. The energy it conducted was raw and wild, threatening to lash out if his focus faltered. But Zarathyn wasn't one to shy from a fight, even with a weapon that seemed just as likely to burn him alive as help him. He squared his shoulders and stepped into the courtyard. The morning air was crisp, the mist lingering around his ankles as if daring him to fail.

He started small. Gripping the staff with both hands, he planted his feet shoulder-width apart and whispered the incantation for a spark. A tiny ember flickered to life at the staff's tip, quivering like a nervous animal. The staff vibrated in his grip, the energy inside it itching to break free. Zarathyn inhaled deeply, steadying himself. With a careful motion, he coaxed the ember to grow, feeding it slivers of his mana. It blossomed into a small flame, steady and controlled.

"Better," he muttered, his voice low and gravelly.

He moved on, pushing the fire into new shapes. The flame stretched into a thread, thin as a spider's silk, before coiling into a sphere. Sweat began to bead on his brow as he worked, his focus unyielding. The sphere spun faster, glowing brighter until he felt the staff's energy begin to buck against him. He clenched his teeth, reining it in with sheer will. Slowly, the flame stabilized, hovering above the staff like a tamed bird.

Zarathyn let the fire dissipate, exhaling as he felt the strain ease. He wasn't done—not by a long shot. Holding the staff horizontally, he began to practice his physical drills. The weapon whirled through the air in wide arcs, the motion stirring the mist at his feet. He twisted his torso with each swing, feeling the muscles in his arms and shoulders strain. The weight of the staff forced him to maintain balance, his feet pivoting on the slick stones to keep him from overextending.

The movements were precise, deliberate. He transitioned seamlessly from an overhead strike to a sweeping horizontal slash, the staff humming faintly with every swing. Each motion was punctuated by a pulse of magic, the staff leaving faint trails of heat in its wake. The air around him grew warmer, the morning mist evaporating as his training intensified.

His breaths came in short bursts now, his chest rising and falling like bellows. Zarathyn pushed harder, driving the staff into the ground with enough force to send a shockwave rippling through the earth. The stone cracked beneath the impact, jagged fissures spidering outward. He followed it with a spinning strike, the staff igniting as he channeled fire through it mid-motion. Flames roared to life, licking at the edges of his vision as he brought the weapon down in a controlled arc.

The energy surged again, threatening to escape. His knuckles whitened as he tightened his grip, forcing the fire to obey. Sweat poured down his face now, stinging his eyes, but he didn't stop. Each swing, each channel of magic, felt like forging steel—grueling and punishing, but worth every drop of effort.

Finally, he let the staff rest. The tip struck the ground with a dull thud, and Zarathyn leaned on it, his chest heaving. The courtyard around him bore the scars of his training—scorched grass, cracked stone, and the faint smell of charred air. His arms ached, his muscles trembling from the strain, but he felt the flicker of pride ignite in his chest.

He wasn't just surviving anymore. He was growing stronger, sharper. The staff was no longer an unpredictable danger—it was a weapon, a tool he was mastering. Zarathyn straightened, gripping the staff tightly.

Tomorrow, he thought, he would push even harder.

CHAPTER 15

Zarathyn sat cross-legged in the artifact room, his back against the cold stone wall. The room was dim, lit only by the faint glow of mana crystals stacked neatly beside him. The soft hum they emitted thrummed in the air, vibrating faintly against his skin like a distant heartbeat. His breath was steady, deliberate, as he stared at the largest crystal in his lap—a jagged hunk of translucent blue that seemed to pulse with raw, unrefined energy. Tonight, he would master it. Or it would break him.

Closing his eyes, Zarathyn began to draw the energy in. It was slow at first, a trickle of power seeping into his body, crawling through his veins like a cautious animal. Then, as he focused, the flow intensified. The power surged forward, crashing into him like a wave. His hands tightened around the crystal as his body tensed, every nerve lighting up as the mana tore through him. It was wild, raw, and unyielding, like trying to tame a storm. His jaw clenched, his breath coming in sharp gasps. For a moment, he felt like he might drown in it.

But he refused to falter. He pulled harder, forcing the energy to obey. His breathing slowed, evening out as he wrestled the surge into submission. In his mind's eye, he visualized the well—a deep, dark reservoir carved into his very being. Its edges were jagged and rough, barely able to contain the torrent of power he fed into it. Every drop of mana filled the space, rippling and swirling with untamed ferocity.

"Steady," he muttered under his breath, his voice barely audible over the hum of energy.

He inhaled deeply, pulling more mana into the well. It roared as it entered, slamming against the walls of his visualization. Cracks appeared along the edges, threatening to spill over. But Zarathyn didn't panic. He focused on his exhale, visualizing the impurities being pushed out. Dark, oily tendrils seeped from the edges of the well, dissipating into nothingness with each controlled breath.

The impurities were more than just stray mana—they were remnants of his own limitations. Doubt. Fear. Hesitation. All of it was purged, leaving the well clearer, stronger. He felt it expand, the walls thickening and stretching to hold more power. Each cycle—inhale, pull, exhale, purge—left him feeling sharper, more in tune with the energy coursing through him.

But it wasn't painless. His muscles trembled, his skin slick with sweat. The mana crystals didn't give their energy willingly; they resisted, as if the essence had a mind of its own. The power pushed back, scraping against his spirit and leaving him raw. His fingers burned where they gripped the crystal, the heat almost unbearable. Still, he held on, feeding the energy into the well and forging it into something greater.

Time slipped away. The glow of the crystals dimmed as he drained them, their once-vivid light fading to a dull flicker. The room felt colder now, the warmth of the mana retreating into his core. The well within him was no longer just a hollow container. It was deeper now, its edges smoothed and fortified, a reservoir that could hold the storm without shattering.

The air in the artifact room tensed as Zarathyn grasped the mana crystal, his fingers pressing into its cool, jagged surface. This one was larger, denser —richer in power than the others he'd drained. He couldn't resist pushing the limits tonight, hungry to test the capacity of his growing well. The crystal pulsed faintly, its light flickering like a trapped flame, almost defiant in its energy. Zarathyn muttered a low incantation, steadying his breathing, and began to pull.

The first surge came fast—too fast. Mana flooded into him, hotter and fiercer than he'd expected, rushing through his veins like molten iron. His heart pounded, his pulse racing in tandem with the flow. He gritted his teeth, sweat beading on his forehead as he fought to maintain control. The crystal resisted, vibrating violently in his hands, but Zarathyn held firm, doubling down on his pull.

The second surge hit like a hammer blow. The crystal cracked, a thin fissure snaking down its center, and the energy inside buckled under the strain. A sudden, high-pitched hum filled the room, the sound climbing higher and higher until it became an ear-splitting shriek. Zarathyn's eyes widened.

"Damn it!" he hissed, releasing the crystal and throwing himself backward.

The explosion came a heartbeat later. A shockwave of unstable mana ripped through the room, slamming into him like a battering ram. Flames licked at his arms, searing through his sleeves and biting into his skin. He hit the ground hard, the impact jarring his spine as chunks of stone and debris rained down from the ceiling. Smoke and the acrid stench of burnt fabric filled the air. His ears rang, drowning out everything else.

Zarathyn rolled onto his side, coughing as he tried to force air back into his lungs. His arms throbbed with pain, the skin red and blistered where the flames had kissed him. He sat up slowly, shaking bits of rubble from his hair, and stared at the remains of the crystal. Or what was left of it. The once-glowing shard was now a pile of jagged shards scattered across the floor, each piece faintly smoking. He cursed under his breath, cradling his burned arm.

But there was no room for pity. Not here. Not now. He forced himself to his feet, staggering slightly as he grabbed onto a nearby pedestal for balance. The room was a mess—singed scrolls, overturned artifacts, soot staining the walls—but it could have been worse. If he hadn't let go when he did, that blast could've gutted him.

"Too greedy," he muttered to himself, flexing his fingers to assess the damage. The burns stung, raw and angry, but they'd heal. What mattered more was the lesson. He'd tried to rip too much too quickly, and the crystal had pushed back. Hard.

He moved toward the next crystal, this one smaller, with a faint green hue, and picked it up gingerly. His palms still tingled with the memory of the explosion. This time, he approached with caution. He steadied his breathing, visualizing the well within himself—not as an empty pit, but as a stream, flowing steadily and evenly. No more floods. No more explosions.

He began to draw again, this time channeling the mana in smaller, controlled streams. The crystal hummed softly, its glow dimming with each pull. Zarathyn focused, letting the energy seep into his well at a steady pace. Each pulse of power was carefully measured, the flow precise and deliberate. His arms ached, the burns pulling at his skin, but he didn't stop. He couldn't afford to.

Minutes stretched into what felt like hours. The green crystal dulled, its light flickering weakly before finally snuffing out. Zarathyn exhaled, his breath shaky but triumphant. He placed the spent crystal onto the ground beside the shattered one, his gaze sharp and determined. The burns on his arms throbbed, the sting a reminder of his failure —but also of his resolve.

"Better," he muttered, brushing soot from his hands. His eyes flicked to the remaining crystals stacked neatly against the far wall.

***

The artifact room glowed faintly in the dim light of Zarathyn's conjured flame, flickering and dancing in his palm. He stared into it, unblinking, his mind grinding through layers of memory like the teeth of a millstone. The fire in his hand wasn't just heat and light—it was control, a weapon, a shield. And right now, it was sloppy. Too wild. Too wasteful. He could hear his old master's voice echoing in his head, sharp and merciless: "A mage who cannot refine his magic might as well fight with a blunt stick."

Zarathyn closed his hand, snuffing the flame out with a hiss. "Not good enough," he muttered, rolling his shoulders. His tunic, already scorched and frayed from days of practice, hung loose on his lean frame. His burns had healed, but the memory of pain lingered like a warning. Still, the only way to grow stronger was to push. Harder. Smarter.

He took a deep breath, letting his mana well up, filling every nerve, every muscle. This time, the flame came sharper. Cleaner. It coiled around him, crackling as it licked the air. He widened his stance, flexing his fingers as the fire spread across his body in a thin, shimmering layer. The heat was immediate, oppressive, like standing too close to a forge. Sweat beaded on his forehead, dripping into his eyes, but he held the shield steady.

The first test came quickly. A jagged piece of debris from his earlier experiments—a shard of broken stone about the size of his fist—lay at his feet. With a flick of his hand, he sent it soaring into the air and hurled himself forward. The stone slammed into the fire shield with a dull thunk, its edges glowing red-hot before bouncing harmlessly to the ground. Zarathyn grinned.

"Closer," he murmured, though the raw sting on his arms told him the shield wasn't perfect yet. Parts of the heat had turned inward, scalding his skin in places where the magic faltered. He couldn't let that happen in a real fight. Adjusting his focus, he channeled more mana, letting the flames tighten around him until they were an almost invisible shimmer. A second shard went flying. This time, it disintegrated on contact, crumbling into ash.

He smirked, flexing his hands, though the victory was short-lived. His skin tingled—raw and blistering where the shield had burned through his focus. The smell of singed fabric wafted up as his tunic smoldered. He tore the ruined sleeve off with a sharp yank, tossing it aside. "Better than nothing," he muttered, rolling his shoulder.

But shields weren't enough. They never had been. Defense would only get you so far. To survive, you had to strike first, strike fast, and strike hard. With that thought, he let the shield collapse, redirecting the flames to his hand. His old training returned in flashes: precise incantations, wrist movements sharper than a blade's edge, the way a good fire spell should feel—solid, cutting, deadly. He began shaping the fire, his mind locking onto a weapon he knew well.

A blade of flame burst to life in his hand, humming with energy. The light painted the walls in shifting shadows as Zarathyn swung it experimentally, the edge searing through the air with a sharp whistle. It wasn't perfect— the flames wavered, their edges flickering and unstable—but it was a start. He gritted his teeth and tried again, pouring more mana into the construct, sharpening its form. This time, the blade solidified, its edges glowing white-hot.

"Not bad," he said under his breath, twirling the blade in a tight arc. The motion felt familiar, almost natural, as if his body still remembered the movements from years ago. He slashed at the air, testing its weight, its balance. Then he turned to the far wall, where a target had been hastily scrawled in soot—a crude circle, just wide enough to simulate an enemy's chest.

Zarathyn pivoted on his heel, the blade carving through the air. The fire hissed as it struck the target dead center, searing through stone and leaving a glowing, jagged scar in its wake. He didn't stop there. With a swift motion, he collapsed the blade, letting the fire coil in his palm before thrusting it forward. A fiery spear exploded from his hand, roaring as it hurtled across the room and slammed into the wall. The impact sent shards of heated stone flying, the spear embedding itself deep before sputtering out in a shower of sparks.

The air hung heavy with smoke and the sharp tang of burning rock. Zarathyn's breathing was ragged, his chest rising and falling as he surveyed the damage. The soot-scrawled target was obliterated, the wall behind it cracked and scorched. He clenched his fists, feeling the mana thrumming beneath his skin. His control was improving, but there was still more to do.

"Not enough," he said, his voice low but steady. His arms ached, his reserves drained, but his eyes burned with determination. The fire was his weapon, his shield, his lifeline. And he would master it, even if it meant tearing himself apart to do it.

The chamber reeked of scorched stone and sweat. Zarathyn crouched low, the tip of his staff pressed against the floor, carving precise lines into the rock. His breathing was steady, though each stroke of the rune demanded absolute focus. A single misstep, one misplaced curve or jagged edge, and the explosion wouldn't just scorch the target—it would obliterate him.

He leaned back, inspecting his work. The rune glowed faintly, its edges shimmering with a dull orange light as his mana seeped into the grooves. It looked simple—a tight cluster of intersecting lines and arcs—but the complexity hummed beneath the surface. Fire runes were dangerous things, volatile by design. They had to be. Precision didn't win battles. Devastation did.

Zarathyn rose, his knees popping like old hinges, and stepped back. The staff's crystal tip still glimmered faintly, heat radiating from where it had etched into the stone. He rolled his shoulders, tightening his grip as he visualized the next steps. A faint smirk tugged at his lips, though it didn't reach his eyes. "Let's see how much hell this thing can raise."

He raised a hand, palm open, and muttered the activation phrase. The words tumbled from his lips like an old chant, steady and rhythmic, spoken more from memory than thought. His fingers curled into a fist, twisting the mana flow as it surged toward the rune. For a moment, nothing happened. Just a faint hiss, the sound of fire licking stone.

hen it erupted.

The rune burst to life, a pillar of flame exploding upward with a deafening boom. Heat slammed into Zarathyn like a fist, forcing him to shield his face with an arm as the fire spiraled skyward, turning the room into a furnace. The force of the blast rippled outward, throwing up debris and rattling the walls. Loose stones clattered to the ground, and the floor beneath the rune glowed red-hot, cracked and smoking.

Zarathyn stumbled back, his boots skidding against the slick stone as the heat seared his skin. A sharp sting danced across his cheek—a piece of shrapnel had grazed him, leaving a thin line of blood trickling down to his jaw. He didn't wipe it away. Instead, he grinned, teeth bared like a predator catching the scent of prey.

"That'll do," he muttered, his voice low and rough, more to himself than anyone else.

He paced around the aftermath, inspecting the damage. The center of the blast zone was obliterated, a blackened crater with edges that still glowed faintly orange. Jagged cracks spiderwebbed outward, reaching nearly to the walls. The destruction wasn't just contained—it spread, unpredictable and wild, just as he'd intended. It wasn't about finesse. It was about fear. Chaos. A fireburst like this wasn't just a weapon—it was a statement.

Still, the aftershocks hummed through his bones, a grim reminder of the risk. The heat in the air clung to him, beads of sweat rolling down his temples and neck. He ran a hand over his face, grimacing as his fingers brushed the shallow cut. It stung, but he ignored it. Pain was part of the process, a necessary price.

He glanced back at the staff, its crystal tip dim now, the residual energy spent. A tool like this wasn't meant for subtlety. It was for carving ruin into the world. Zarathyn crouched again, his eyes narrowing as he traced a finger along the edge of the rune's remains. The grooves were blackened, warped by the sheer force of the explosion. It had worked, but the output was inefficient. Too much wasted energy in the edges. The next one would have to be tighter. Sharper.

He straightened, his gaze hardening as he surveyed the chamber. Already, ideas churned in his mind—how to make the runes more compact, how to chain the bursts together for a sustained barrage. He could see it clearly: a battlefield littered with these symbols, each one a ticking time bomb. Enemies would hesitate, unsure where to step, and in that hesitation, they'd burn.

But for now, there was only the empty room, the scorched stone, and the lingering heat. Zarathyn twirled the staff once, its crystal flashing faintly as he adjusted his grip. He stepped to another patch of floor, unmarked and pristine. There was no pause, no hesitation. He knelt and began carving again, the lines sharp, deliberate, each stroke a promise of destruction.

CHAPTER 16

The stones didn't give him much choice—they were jagged, awkward, and unyielding. Zarathyn liked that. Smooth edges were for luxuries he no longer had. His hands, rough and calloused from weeks of this routine, wrapped around the largest piece of rubble he could find. It was a chunk of old masonry, uneven and riddled with sharp edges that bit into his palms when he lifted it.

With a sharp exhale, he hoisted the stone above his head. His muscles strained, veins bulging against his forearms as he locked his elbows. The weight dragged on his shoulders, a dull ache settling deep in his bones, but he held firm. Each second was a test of will as much as strength. The air was thick with dust, stirred up by his movements and clinging to the sweat dripping from his temples.

He dropped the stone with a heavy thud that echoed through the ruined chamber. The floor shuddered under its weight, cracks spiderwebbing out beneath it. Zarathyn flexed his fingers, shaking out the stiffness, and moved to another piece of rubble. This one was smaller but still formidable—

hefting it in one hand, he pressed it overhead, then lowered it to his shoulder. Back and forth, over and over, until his arms screamed for relief.

"Not yet," he muttered, his voice little more than a growl. He adjusted his grip, forcing himself to push through the burn. Pain meant progress. He wasn't going to let a body softened by weeks of decay hold him back.

When his arms felt like lead and his shoulders throbbed with every heartbeat, he shifted to his next exercise. He ran, weaving through the ruined halls of the castle. The air was cooler here, shadows pooling in every corner, but the floor was treacherous. Fallen beams and jagged chunks of stone littered his path. He darted around them, his steps quick and deliberate, dodging the obstacles with a dancer's precision.

At one point, a loose slab of rock shifted underfoot. Zarathyn stumbled, catching himself with one hand before he could hit the ground. His palm scraped against the rough surface, leaving behind a smear of blood. He hissed but didn't stop, didn't even slow. He pushed harder, sprinting now, his breathing ragged as his boots pounded against the uneven floor.

As he neared the end of the hallway, he jumped —not a simple leap, but something far more dangerous. Fire burst beneath his feet, a controlled explosion that sent him soaring higher than any normal jump could. The flames licked at the soles of his boots, their heat barely contained as he propelled himself forward. For a moment, he hung in the air, weightless and unshackled, before gravity dragged him back down.

He landed with a roll, his body tucking instinctively to absorb the impact. The floor groaned beneath him, loose debris scattering as he skidded to a halt. He stood, dusting off his tunic, and glanced back at the scorched imprint where he'd launched himself. It was crude, messy—but effective. The technique wasn't perfect yet, but it would get there.

Again.

This time, Zarathyn focused on control. As he jumped, he funneled just enough mana into the fireburst to lift him without scorching the floor. He adjusted mid-air, angling his body for a smoother descent, and landed with a precision that was almost surgical. The impact jarred his knees, but it was cleaner, sharper. Progress.

By the time he finished, his lungs burned, and his legs felt like they'd been replaced with iron weights. He leaned against a crumbling column, sweat dripping from his chin as he caught his breath. The castle was silent, save for the faint creak of settling ruins and the distant rustle of wind through broken windows.

Zarathyn wiped the blood from his scraped palm onto his tunic, smearing it into the fabric, and glanced at the rubble-strewn path he'd just carved through. His body ached, his mana reserves were low, and his muscles screamed for rest—but his lips twisted into a grim smile.

He wasn't done yet. Not by a long shot.

***

Zarathyn stood in the middle of the courtyard, the battered stone underfoot slick with a mix of sweat and the dust kicked up by his constant movement. He felt the weight of the staff in his hands, steady now, more a part of him than a tool. The crystal at its tip caught the dim light of the fading day, flashing with a pulse of latent power. He was no longer the mage who once summoned torrents of flame from thin air; that power had been stripped away, broken and fractured, until now he had to rebuild it, piece by agonizing piece.

The first strike came without warning—a heavy swing, a defensive arc meant to bat aside an imaginary blade. The staff whistled through the air as it connected with the non-existent threat, a crackle of force vibrating up his arms. His feet shifted in response, the fluid movement a practiced dance. His breath was even, controlled, a stark contrast to the wild thrashing of his younger self when he'd first started these drills.

Before his opponent could recover, he was already moving again, his free hand snapping out in a sharp motion. Fire. His fingers traced the familiar gestures, a burst of heat surging from his palm and slamming into the air ahead of him. The bolt streaked through the space, slicing the silence with a crackle that made the hairs on his neck stand up. The force of it sent a ripple through his body, a wave of power that vibrated in his core. His body hummed with it—both physical and magical strength bound in the same heartbeat.

He spun low this time, ducking under an imagined sword swipe, the staff coming down in a brutal counterstrike. The impact reverberated through his arm, but he barely flinched. The staff slammed into the ground, its arc sweeping the air around him like a protective circle. No attack would slip past him. Not now.

His other hand followed. Fire again. This time, the bolt was faster, sharper. He snapped it into the air like a whip, the pulse of magic bursting from his palm with a sound like thunder breaking. The force of it hit the wall with a sickening crack, the stone cracking and splitting as though it had been hit by a boulder. Bits of rock exploded outward, some small shards lodging into his tunic. He didn't flinch. Blood trickled from a fresh cut on his shoulder.

"Better," Zarathyn muttered, gritting his teeth. He wiped the blood away with the back of his hand, ignoring the sting. He wasn't here for comfort. Not anymore. Not when every move had to count. Not when survival meant perfecting this deadly combination of staff and fire.

He lunged forward next, sweeping the staff upward, the long shaft cutting through the air like a spear. Fire exploded from his palm in a smooth wave, rolling from his fingertips in a stream of heat that threatened to burn the air itself. He struck again, with the staff, driving it in hard and fast, almost instinctively. A bolt of fire followed as his body moved with the fluidity of someone who had lived this for years. He could feel the magic starting to sync with his every motion— his strikes were no longer independent, but part of something bigger, something greater.

The next motion was a leap. He surged forward, using his staff to vault into the air. Mid-flight, he unleashed another bolt, a stream of fire that followed his body's momentum. The air crackled around him, the heat blistering his skin, but he didn't care. He was already landing, already sweeping his staff again, the arc cutting through the imaginary enemy's defense with a sickening crunch. He could almost hear the bones snap in his mind's eye.

His heart hammered in his chest, the sound deafening as the world around him seemed to blur, everything revolving around the dance of combat and the rush of power. He felt the fire in his veins, the magic surging just as it had in the old days. But now it was tempered, shaped by his fists, his will, and the harsh reality that each strike could be the difference between life and death. There was no time for hesitation, no time for second-guessing. Just action.

Zarathyn's breath came in ragged bursts, sweat streaming down his face, mixing with the grime and blood already caking his skin. Every strike, every bolt, every movement was raw. He pushed through the exhaustion, through the ache of muscles he hadn't used in so long, until the sweat burned in his eyes and the pain sharpened his focus.

The ground was scorched beneath him now, patches of blackened earth where fire had landed. The air around him was thick with smoke and the crackle of fading embers. He let the staff fall to the ground, its heavy end digging into the earth, as he caught his breath. His pulse still thundered in his ears, his chest heaving with the effort.

He wiped his face, leaving another streak of red across his forehead as he straightened up.

"Not bad," he murmured to himself, eyes narrowing as he stared at the devastation around him. The power felt good, but he knew it wasn't enough. Not yet. Not until he could make it a weapon. A weapon that killed.

Zarathyn exhaled sharply. There was more to do. Always more.

CHAPTER 17

Zarathyn hunched over the stone floor, his hands shaking with anticipation, or maybe it was from the weight of his failure. He hadn't done this in years—not since before everything had come crashing down, not since he'd been reduced to a shadow of his former self. But the scrolls had shown him a glimpse, an ancient technique just beyond his reach. Summoning. Elementals. It was a spell he'd never fully mastered before, a step too far even for someone who'd danced with forces others could only imagine. But now? Now he had no choice but to try.

The chamber was silent except for the low crackle of the fire in the corner, its flickering light casting long shadows across the floor. The air felt thick, pressing against his skin like the weight of all the mistakes he'd made. He couldn't afford another failure. Not here. Not like this.

With steady hands, he scattered powdered crystal across the cold stone, the fine dust catching the light and swirling in slow spirals. His fingers trembled—whether from the effort, the hunger for power, or something else, he couldn't say. The lines he drew with the crystal were precise, each one traced with the kind of care that only years of magical training could instill. A circle. A seal. The elements would obey.

As he completed the final strokes, Zarathyn stepped back and drew in a slow breath, his body tight with the effort to hold back the flood of memories that threatened to overwhelm him. There was no room for that right now. Not when the circle was still fresh, still intact. The magic hummed, faint at first, but unmistakable. It was alive. Waiting.

His hand fell to the ground, his palm flat against the cold stone. The chant started as a low murmur, words he'd committed to memory from the scrolls. Old words, ancient words. As he spoke them, they tasted like ash in his mouth, their power rippling through him, sinking into the very marrow of his bones. His breath quickened, matching the rise of energy around him.

For a moment, nothing happened. He'd expected that. Summoning was never a clean, easy thing. But he could feel it—the shift in the air, the crackle in the stone beneath him. The ground groaned under his feet, a faint tremor running through the earth, and then—boom—a burst of force ripped through the chamber. The circle flared bright, and the room filled with heat.

Zarathyn's heart slammed into his chest as a figure began to take shape in the center of the circle. A column of fire twisted upward, roaring like a beast awakened. Flames licked the air, curling around the outline of a figure, an elemental of pure fire. The heat was unbearable, scorching the air, burning the hairs on his arms. Sweat stung his eyes, but he didn't move, didn't look away. The elemental's shape solidified, a towering mass of flame, its edges flickering and shifting, as if it were made of living fire itself.

Zarathyn's heart thundered in his chest as the creature's eyes—if it had eyes—locked onto him. The air grew thick with power. The elemental's heat was oppressive, crushing, a pressure that made it hard to breathe, like standing too close to the heart of a furnace.

But this was no time to admire his handiwork. He didn't know how long the summoning would hold, how long he could keep this creature bound to his will. He had to make it obey. He forced his hands steady, his voice strong, reciting the words of command. The magic surged with each syllable, each command, but the elemental didn't flinch. Didn't obey. It swirled in place, a swirling storm of flame, as if it were deciding whether to rip his face off or listen to him.

He could feel the temperature rise—no, roar—as the elemental took a step forward. Heat crashed into him like a wave, burning the air, scorching the stone beneath his feet. The pressure in his chest tightened. His lungs burned. His skin prickled, the heat threatening to blister him alive.

Zarathyn gritted his teeth and pressed on.

Focus. Control. His voice cracked through the roar of the elemental's fury. "Obey me."

Another burst of flame. A fiery hand, far too large, swung through the air toward him. The fire was alive, a raging thing, a monster freed from the cage of magic. He was already moving, rolling to the side, narrowly avoiding the blast of flame that singed the air where he'd just been standing. The stone floor beneath him cracked with the force of the attack, and he felt the heat lick at his back as he scrambled to his feet.

This wasn't supposed to happen. He hadn't prepared for this level of chaos. But the elemental was not cooperating, and it was only a matter of time before it tore the chamber apart if he couldn't get it under control.

His thoughts raced. Control it. Bind it. Finish the ritual. He raised his staff, its crystal tip glowing faintly in the flames' light, and cast another binding rune, slamming it into the air with a shout. The fire elemental howled, a sound like a hundred infernos screaming at once, as if the room itself was going to explode under the force of its rage.

Zarathyn's pulse hammered in his ears as he fought to hold the ritual together. His hands bled from the effort, cuts opening along his palms where the magic had torn into him. The pain was raw, but it wasn't the pain that mattered. It was the power. He couldn't let it slip. Not now.

With one last breath, he poured all of his

remaining strength into the binding. His body felt like it was burning from the inside out, but it was working. The elemental was shrinking, forced back into the circle, pushed and bound by his will. The flames flickered and snapped, but Zarathyn's command cut through them. The fire flared one last time, then slowly began to die, leaving only the faintest glow behind.

Exhausted, bleeding, and covered in sweat, Zarathyn staggered back, his breath ragged. The elemental was gone—its presence a smoldering residue in the air. But the lesson had been learned: the power he sought was not something to be taken lightly. This ritual, this control, would require more than brute force. It would require patience. Precision. And most of all, it would demand his will.

***

Zarathyn stood before the circle, his breath steady, his mind focused. The air was thick with anticipation, and his heart beat in time with the magical hum that buzzed under his skin. The fire elemental had slipped through his grasp once, had torn at the edges of his will, but he wasn't going to let that happen again. Not this time. He had learned. He had adapted. The runes were laid out on the stone floor, powdered crystal marking their intricate paths. The incantation was fresh in his mind—each word, each gesture, ingrained in his very bones.

This time, it would work.

With a fluid motion, he placed his hand on the ground and began the chant. It rolled from his tongue with more power than before, an unbroken line of command that surged into the circle. The runes pulsed, flaring like embers catching flame, and then—boom. The ground trembled, dust falling from the ceiling as the elemental tore through the circle, a mass of fire and rage, its form flickering at first, uncertain, but growing stronger with each passing moment.

Zarathyn didn't move. His eyes locked onto the towering figure of flame, its body a writhing inferno, its molten eyes burning with a hunger all their own. He could feel the heat of it, the oppressive weight of its presence pressing down on him, like standing too close to the heart of a volcano. But this time, he was ready. This time, he had control.

The creature loomed over him, a humanoid figure made entirely of fire, its edges licking at the air like the tongues of some ancient beast. Heat radiated off of it in waves, warping the air around them, but Zarathyn stood firm. His will was iron now, not the quivering thing it had been before.

"Stand," Zarathyn commanded, his voice a sharp, commanding force. The elemental's form stilled for a moment before it obeyed, taking a step forward. It was not a mere flame now; it was something more, something he controlled, something that bent to his will.

He tested it. "Lift that stone," he ordered, gesturing to the large boulder in the corner of the chamber. The elemental's body crackled and roared as it reached toward the stone, its fiery hands wrapping around it, lifting it with ease. The stone groaned under the heat, its surface beginning to crack, but the elemental held it steady, its molten form unwavering. Zarathyn nodded, satisfaction flashing in his eyes.

But his victory was short-lived. He felt it then —a drain on his mana, sharp and insistent, like a blade scraping against bone. His breath hitched, and for the briefest moment, the elemental's flame flickered, its form wavered as if it might collapse. Zarathyn's hand shot out, gripping the mana crystal at his belt. He felt its power pulse through him, a sudden surge of energy that coursed through his veins like a flood.

He cycled the energy, pulling from the crystal, feeding it into his own body. The mana slid into him, rushing through his bloodstream, filling the empty spaces that the elemental's presence had drained. His focus narrowed, and with a thought, he pushed the crystal's energy into the elemental, stabilizing it once more.

The fire roared again, its molten eyes blazing with intensity, but it held firm. Zarathyn's heart raced, but he kept the flow steady, ensuring the elemental didn't slip from his control.

"Good," he murmured, more to himself than anything else. The heat from the creature's body felt like a furnace at his back, but he could handle it. His hands shook with the effort, but he held his ground.

The elemental moved again, following his command without hesitation, but Zarathyn could feel the toll it was taking. His mana reserves were slipping fast. The surge from the crystal wasn't enough. He had to be careful. He had to be precise.

"Enough," he said, his voice strained. The elemental stilled at his command, its fiery body crackling, the air around them thick with the scent of scorched earth. Zarathyn staggered back, his head swimming from the effort. The pressure of maintaining the elemental was intense, the drain on his mana far greater than he had anticipated. His muscles burned, and sweat beaded on his brow, but he didn't allow himself a moment of weakness. He had succeeded. The creature obeyed. He had done it.

The elemental's flames sputtered, but it remained steady, its eyes locked onto him with an intelligence that made the hairs on his neck stand on end. Zarathyn clenched his fists, drawing in another deep breath. He would not falter. He had learned his lesson. He would master this.

But for now, he allowed himself a moment of victory—brief, fleeting. The elemental was his. And with it, so was the power.

CHAPTER 18

Zarathyn's confidence grew with each summon. What had once been a difficult and unpredictable act now felt as natural as breathing. The runes —those complex, swirling patterns of power—had become a crutch, something he no longer needed. He could call them forth with nothing more than the heat of his will and a few sharp words. It was a step forward, and it felt good.

He began with the small ones, the lesser elementals. Nothing more than flickers of flame, wisps of air, or shifting patches of earth. They were perfect for training, for honing his skills. They moved like wildfire, darting in and out of the shadows, testing his reflexes, forcing him to keep his mind sharp. But even the smallest of them was dangerous, relentless in their assaults. And Zarathyn was only too glad to oblige them.

His staff whipped through the air in sharp arcs, his strikes cutting through the dust and smoke. Fireballs burst from his hands, crashing against the elemental's shifting form, but it didn't give. It howled—if such a thing could be said to howl— and charged again, claws of fire reaching for him.

Zarathyn reacted fast, twisting his body and leaping to the side just as the elemental's claws raked the air where he'd stood. He could feel the heat from the attack, the searing intensity of the flames licking at his skin. Sweat slicked his brow, but his movements were quick, deliberate. He wasn't just dodging; he was anticipating.

The elemental was fast, but Zarathyn was faster. With a sharp twist of his staff, he thrust it forward, conjuring a wall of flame to stop the elemental's charge. The creature screeched as it was forced back, its form rippling and warping under the heat. But it didn't retreat for long.

Zarathyn's heart pounded, his breath steady as he prepared for the next move. He could feel the battle in his bones, the rhythm of it, and he liked it. He liked it too much.

He conjured another elemental. This one was bigger—darker, more aggressive. The air thickened with heat as it took form, its fiery body crackling and snapping. Zarathyn wasn't afraid. Not anymore. He had learned how to bend them to his will. Or so he thought.

The battle shifted. The new elemental broke free faster than he could react, its fiery body surging forward in a violent rush, faster than any of the others. It slashed at him with ferocious speed, burning the air around him. Zarathyn threw up a barrier of fire to block the first strike, but the elemental was too quick. It ripped through his defense like paper, its claws catching the edge of his tunic, shredding the fabric and sending pain shooting through his side. He stumbled, barely managing to hold his ground as the creature pressed in.

This wasn't just training anymore. This was a fight for his life.

His heart raced as the elemental came for him again. This time, it wasn't just attacking—it was trying to kill. Its molten claws dug into the stone floor as it closed the gap between them. Zarathyn cursed under his breath, throwing himself to the side as the elemental's fiery hands missed by inches.

A surge of panic ripped through him, but he tamped it down. He had dealt with worse—he had been the worst. With a growl, he gathered the power around him. His fingers twitched, sending pulses of magic into the air, shaping the flames into sharp tendrils that reached for the elemental, trying to ensnare it.

The elemental howled again, thrashing against his control. It was too strong, too wild. He couldn't keep it bound.

The air in the chamber was thick with heat now, the walls sweating under the pressure. Zarathyn's mana was running low, and he could feel the weariness in his bones, the gnawing hunger for energy. He needed to end this, and fast.

With a growl, he shifted his stance and slammed his staff into the ground, using the force of the impact to channel the magic. He could feel the arcane energies gathering in his core, coiling like a snake ready to strike. He focused, concentrating all of his will into one final burst.

The explosion of power sent shockwaves through the room. The elemental screeched as the binding spell wrapped around it, forcing its movements to slow. Zarathyn pressed harder, forcing the flames to bend to his will. He could feel the creature's resistance, the crackling, burning fury of it, but he didn't give an inch.

With a final, deafening roar, the elemental's form flickered, its body collapsing in on itself, the flames snuffing out like a candle being blown out in the wind. The air turned cold, and the room was silent except for Zarathyn's ragged breathing.

He stood there, chest heaving, sweat dripping down his face. His side burned where the claws had torn through, but the pain was distant, a reminder of how close he had come to failure. He wiped the blood from his lip, his hands shaking.

That was too close. Much too close.

But he had won. And in that victory, something within him shifted. He was no longer just the mage who summoned fire—he was the one who commanded it. The one who controlled it.

And the elemental? It had learned its place.

***

Weeks bled into one another in a blur of sweat, blood, and fire. Zarathyn could feel it now, the change crawling beneath his skin, settling into his bones. It wasn't just the physical strain of training, the endless days of hunting or toiling with magic that had worn him down. It was something else —a sharpening of the senses, a razor edge honed from constant testing. His body had become something tighter, stronger, more attuned to the world around him. His muscles, once stiff from disuse, rippled with a raw, violent power. He felt faster, more alive with every breath, as though the air itself conspired to help him tear through the world.

But it wasn't just the physical. His magic had grown. It no longer flickered or sputtered; it roared. Every spell was smoother, more precise. His hands could call flames with a thought, twist the earth with a whisper. The long hours of practice had paid off in ways that felt almost... unnatural. He wasn't just a man who used magic now. He was magic, and it surged through him with every beat of his heart.

This morning, like every morning, he stood in the center of the chamber, eyes locked on the target—a small, flame elemental dancing at his side, its fiery form flickering with life. The air was thick with heat, crackling with energy as his staff gleamed with a molten glow, the tip shimmering with the concentrated power of his magic. The chamber was silent but for the crackling of the elemental's fire, and the pulse of his own heartbeat, steady and calm.

His grip on the staff tightened as he felt the

familiar spark of power flare in his chest. The elemental swirled in place, its molten form barely containing the chaos within it. A controlled chaos. He had learned to mold that fire into something useful, something deadly.

He thrust his staff forward, feeling the magic rush to meet his will. The elemental followed his command, darting through the air with speed and precision. It swiped through the room like a living storm, its flickering tendrils of flame licking the stone walls, but Zarathyn was already moving, his feet dancing across the ground. No more hesitation, no more wasted motion.

Each step flowed into the next. His staff spun in fluid arcs, a seamless extension of his body as he blocked and countered, the elemental's fire slamming against his magical barriers, leaving behind only scorch marks on the stone. The heat from the impact sent a familiar burn through his veins, but it wasn't pain—it was power. He was using it, feeding on it. This wasn't about avoiding the damage. It was about embracing it.

The elemental lunged again, its molten body expanding, surging with fury. But Zarathyn had already anticipated the move. He rolled forward, dodging under its flaming claws, and in the same motion, hurled a pulse of magic straight at its center. The explosion of fire sent a wave of heat crashing into him, but he barely flinched. His body had been forged in this crucible, and the heat didn't touch him anymore. His magic, his control, had surpassed the wildness of the flames.

As the elemental faltered, staggered by the blast, Zarathyn pressed forward. He could feel his mana reserves drain with every movement, every burst of power, but it didn't matter. Not now. He had learned to draw from the crystals, to channel the raw energy of the earth itself into his body, into his magic. He was becoming more than what he'd been before. This was what he'd trained for. This was the end of being the hunted.

The elemental's form flickered again, its fire dimming just enough to signal its weakening. It was still alive, still dangerous, but it was no longer a threat. Zarathyn's magic surged one final time, spiraling outward in a brilliant arc of flame, engulfing the elemental in a burst of controlled destruction. The creature's fiery body crumpled under the force, its flames sputtering and dying out in a hiss of smoke.

Zarathyn stood in the center of the chamber, chest heaving, his staff still glowing with residual power. He felt the quiet thrum of his magic settling in his veins, the sweat on his skin cool against the wind he had summoned. The room was scorched and broken, but he didn't care. The battle was over, and for the first time in weeks, he felt it—the stirrings of triumph.

The forest, with its brutal, unyielding threats, still lurked just beyond the stone walls. He knew that. He wasn't deluded enough to think he'd mastered everything. There were dangers out there, and plenty of them. But for the first time, Zarathyn didn't fear them.

He was no longer the prey, the one running from whatever terror the wilds could throw at him.

He was becoming the predator.

CHAPTER 19

Zarathyn crouched on the jagged hilltop, the cold wind tugging at his cloak as he studied the facility below. It sprawled across the valley like a festering wound on the land, a fortress of arcane steel and glimmering mana crystals. Streams of blue light pulsed through conduits along the walls, feeding the monstrous machines inside. Even from this distance, he could feel the hum of power vibrating in his bones—a symphony of raw mana twisted to fuel weapons of domination.

The facility wasn't just a factory; it was a forge of tyranny. Mana-powered cannons bristled along the perimeter walls, their crystal cores glowing faintly in the dim light. They could vaporize anything within range with a single burst of energy. Above, drones buzzed in lazy circuits, their sleek forms inscribed with glowing runes that pulsed as they scanned the area. Guards patrolled in synchronized movements, clad in mana-enhanced armor that shimmered faintly with protective wards. Their weapons—crossbows reinforced with glowing mana conduits—looked sleek and deadly, each bolt tipped with a shard of energy that could pierce through steel.

Zarathyn's gaze shifted to the massive domed structure at the heart of the compound. It gleamed like a dark jewel, its surface etched with runes that pulsed faintly, cycling mana through its structure. He could feel it from here: the nexus. That was the heart of the beast, the core that powered everything. If he could destroy it, the entire facility would collapse in on itself, taking their precious war machines with it.

He clenched his staff, its gnarled wood warm under his hand as it responded to his energy. Sparks flickered along its length, faint but eager, the fire within him ready to be unleashed. But not yet. He wasn't a fool who'd rush headlong into a meat grinder. The Dominium's arrogance was its greatest weakness. They believed their machines and wards made them untouchable. He'd prove them wrong.

Zarathyn crouched lower, studying the patrol patterns. The perimeter was guarded by sentry golems, hulking constructs powered by mana cores embedded deep in their chests. Their movements were precise, almost fluid, a stark contrast to the lumbering machines of old. Each step sent a faint ripple of energy through the ground as they scanned for intruders. Further in, mana-forged mechs stood in idle rows, their massive limbs bristling with integrated weaponry. These weren't just machines; they were weapons of war, designed to crush rebellion and sow terror.

His eyes narrowed as he traced the weaknesses in their defenses. The turrets rotated with clockwork precision, but their targeting runes had blind spots at the edges of their arcs. The drones' scanning fields overlapped, but only barely. And the sentry golems, for all their precision, moved in predictable patterns. The Dominium relied too much on their technology, thinking it made them invincible. They hadn't accounted for someone like him—someone who could see the cracks in their perfection.

He extended a hand, palm up, and summoned a flicker of flame. It coiled and twisted in his grasp, a living thing that reflected the fire in his golden eyes. He whispered a command, and the flame leapt from his hand, forming into a small, darting elemental. The creature shimmered as it absorbed his intent, its body crackling with energy. Without hesitation, it darted forward, weaving through the shadows like a hunter on the prowl.

Zarathyn watched it go, his gaze steady. The elemental would scout ahead, finding the best points of entry and the most vulnerable targets. Meanwhile, he took a moment to center himself. The air here was thick with mana, tainted by the Dominium's machines. It buzzed around him, wild and hungry, but he drew it in anyway, channeling it through his body. It burned like fire in his veins, but he welcomed the pain. It reminded him of what he was fighting for.

His attention shifted to the workers visible

through the factory's glass walls. They moved like shadows, their shoulders hunched and their movements stiff. Prisoners, no doubt, forced to toil under the Dominium's watchful gaze. He could see the lines of exhaustion etched into their faces even from this distance. They were little more than cogs in the machine, their lives consumed to feed the war effort.

He tightened his grip on his staff, the wood thrumming with his magic. These people might not even realize he was here to free them—or that freedom would come wrapped in flames and ruin. But that didn't matter. The Dominium's hold over them would end tonight.

The elemental returned, its body flickering excitedly as it communicated what it had found. Zarathyn closed his eyes, letting the creature's impressions flood his mind: a gap in the patrols near the western gate, a blind spot in the drones' paths, and a weak point in the facility's outer wall where the mana conduits ran close to the surface. Perfect.

He rose to his feet, his cloak swirling around him as the wind picked up. The facility glowed below, a beacon of oppression against the darkened landscape. But by the time the sun rose, it would be nothing more than a smoldering ruin.

"Let's see how well your mana machines hold up against the real thing," Zarathyn muttered, his voice low and sharp. The fire in his staff flared briefly, reflecting the grim determination in his eyes.

He descended the hill, his movements silent and deliberate. The Dominium thought they had built an impenetrable fortress. Zarathyn would show them the flaw in their design. One way or another, the beast would bleed.

Zarathyn crouched in the underbrush, his cloak blending seamlessly into the night. The metallic hum of mana engines vibrated through the air, faint but insistent, like an unwelcome heartbeat. Below him, the facility sprawled in rigid lines, its walls of steel and arcane conduits forming a maze of industry and malice. Blue mana conduits pulsed faintly, casting an otherworldly glow on the patrols moving in careful rhythms around the perimeter.

He tightened his grip on his staff, the polished wood thrumming faintly with power. A sharp spark of fire flickered to life in his palm, eager to be unleashed, but he extinguished it with a slow exhale. Not yet. Charging in with flames blazing might feel satisfying, but it'd be suicide against a fortress this fortified. No, this required precision.

His golden eyes tracked the movements of the guards below. They were outfitted in mana-infused armor, the plates shimmering faintly with protective wards. Each carried a mana crossbow slung across their back, the glowing bolts in their quivers promising a painful, likely fatal end to anything they hit. Between the guards, insectile drones hovered in careful patterns, their sleek frames humming softly as mana cores thrummed at their centers. Every so often, their scanning runes flared, casting beams of light that swept the area.

Zarathyn leaned back, pressing his body against the rough bark of a gnarled tree. The Dominium relied so much on their machines and their patterns, their calculated order. He'd exploit that. He extended a hand, palm up, and summoned a flicker of flame. The fire swirled and twisted, coalescing into a small, darting elemental. The creature hovered for a moment, its form flickering with eager energy, before Zarathyn gave it a subtle command.

"Go," he murmured, his voice low and firm.

The elemental streaked forward like a hunting fox, its flame dimming as it flitted through the shadows. Zarathyn watched it go, his senses extended outward, feeling the faint heat it left in its wake. The creature darted between the gaps in the metallic walls, squeezing through tight spaces with fluid precision. It paused just inside the perimeter, observing the patrol routes before continuing deeper into the facility.

Zarathyn closed his eyes, letting the elemental's impressions filter back to him. It wasn't language, exactly—more like bursts of heat and flickers of light that translated into shapes and movements in his mind. He saw the western gate, the weakest point in the wall where the mana conduits ran shallow. He felt the heat of a patrol moving too close to a blind spot, their steps too regimented to account for the chaos of real combat. He sensed the rhythmic pulse of a larger mana core buried deep in the facility, its power humming through every machine and weapon within.

The elemental returned, streaking back to Zarathyn with a crackle of heat. It circled his head once, its tiny form flaring brightly, before vanishing into a wisp of smoke. Zarathyn opened his eyes, the rough map of the facility now burned into his mind. He smirked grimly.

"Arrogant bastards," he muttered, his voice low and sharp. "You've built your fortress out of patterns. Let's see how it holds up to chaos."

He adjusted his cloak, pulling it tighter around his shoulders, and rose silently from his crouch. The mana engines thrummed louder now, as though the facility itself sensed what was coming. Zarathyn's staff pulsed faintly in his grip, the fire within it restless but controlled.

Every step he took was deliberate, his movements as fluid and precise as a predator stalking its prey. The guards below had no idea what was coming. Their machines couldn't sense him, their scanning patterns couldn't predict him. Zarathyn had lived through centuries of war and conquest, had wielded powers they couldn't begin to comprehend. And now, he would remind them why the world once trembled at his name.

He paused at the edge of the tree line, his

eyes locked on the western gate. It was time to turn their fortress of patterns into a monument of failure.

With a flick of his wrist, Zarathyn conjured another small flame, letting it coil lazily around his fingers before he extinguished it. The time for reconnaissance was over. Now came the firestorm.

CHAPTER 20

The moment had arrived. Zarathyn crouched at the edge of the tree line, his sharp eyes locked on the facility's perimeter. The patrol drones hovered with eerie precision, their mana cores pulsing faintly like heartbeats in the still night. Each emitted a pale blue beam, sweeping the ground in slow, deliberate arcs. Their creators probably thought them flawless. Zarathyn's lips curled into a faint, humorless smile. They were wrong.

With a deep breath, he drew on his magic. It surged through him, crackling and alive, infusing his muscles and joints. His body felt lighter, stronger, like a coiled spring waiting to explode into motion. He pushed off the ground, his movements eerily silent, a blur of controlled speed and raw power as he sprinted across the open terrain. His cloak flared briefly behind him, then settled as he crouched low, moving with the practiced precision of someone who had once commanded legions.

A faint hum cut through the air, sharp and growing louder. Zarathyn froze mid-step, instincts flaring. A drone whirred closer, its scanning beam sweeping dangerously near. He dropped to the cold, hard ground in a single fluid motion, his body pressed against the dirt. The mana-charged blue light grazed past, lighting up the area mere inches from his face.

Zarathyn muttered an incantation under his breath, a few clipped, ancient words that felt foreign in the mechanical world around him. Heat shimmered into existence, forming a thin veil around his prone body. The distortion rippled faintly, bending light and obscuring him like a mirage in the desert. He kept still, forcing his breathing into shallow, controlled gulps as the drone hovered just above him.

It lingered, its beam lingering on a patch of grass that swayed slightly from his passing. For a tense moment, the hum grew louder, the mana core within the drone thrumming with barely contained energy. Zarathyn's hand twitched, his fingers aching to send a firebolt straight through the machine's heart. But no. Patience.

Finally, the drone moved on, its light fading into the distance. Zarathyn waited another heartbeat, then let the heat veil dissipate with a soft hiss of steam. He pushed off the ground, silent as a shadow, and resumed his advance.

The wall loomed ahead, a cold expanse of reinforced steel etched with glowing runes that thrummed faintly with protective wards. No matter. His magic could crack those protections like brittle stone. He took a moment to gauge the distance, his eyes flicking up to the smooth, unbroken surface.

Zarathyn extended one hand, summoning a controlled burst of fire around his feet. The heat surged beneath him, propelling him upward in a fiery leap. His fingers latched onto the edge of a narrow seam in the wall, the steel searing hot from his magic, but his grip held firm. The wards shimmered faintly where his hand touched, struggling to resist his presence, but he poured fire into them. The runes sputtered and died, their light snuffed out like candles in a storm.

With a grunt, he swung his body upward, using the momentum to scale higher. His staff, slung across his back, vibrated faintly as if eager to be used, but he ignored it for now. His next jump took him to a ledge near the top of the wall, where he perched briefly, scanning the interior.

The facility stretched before him, its angular corridors and glowing conduits a stark contrast to the natural darkness outside. Patrols moved in pairs below, their mana-imbued armor glinting faintly under the arcane lighting. Drones buzzed overhead, but their scanning patterns were predictable, methodical. Zarathyn grinned. Machines didn't adapt. He did.

He crouched, muscles tensed, and prepared to descend. The game had begun, and the Dominium didn't even know it yet.

The facility swallowed him whole, a beast of metal and mana. The walls pulsed faintly

CRAIG ZERF

with arcane conduits, blue light coursing through transparent tubes embedded in the steel. The air tasted of iron and burnt mana, thick and cloying. The hum of machinery was an ever-present growl, a reminder that this place was alive in its own way, though utterly devoid of soul. Zarathyn hated it immediately.

He crouched low, pressing himself against a column as the hiss of pressurized steam erupted from a nearby pipe. Conveyor belts rattled on either side of him, carrying raw mana crystals and enchanted alloys to forges glowing white-hot. The workers here weren't people, not really —automatons with crude human forms shuffled between stations, their arms a mess of exposed gears and runes. Occasionally, a flesh-and-blood technician would appear, issuing commands or fine-tuning the machinery. None of them had faces worth remembering.

Zarathyn let the staff in his hand pulse with the faintest flicker of magic. He channeled the energy carefully, weaving it into a subtle distortion that masked him from the mechanical eyes swiveling above. Security cameras tracked the area in rigid patterns, their lenses glowing like hungry insects. The Dominium believed in their machines more than their people. That would be their undoing.

A lone technician wandered too close, clipboard in hand and eyes glued to the glowing readings of a tablet. He didn't even glance up, his path intersecting with Zarathyn's hiding spot behind a stack of mana cores. Zarathyn moved like a wraith, his steps silent on the grated floor. His free hand lashed out, catching the technician's head in a vice-like grip. A precise blow to the temple with the butt of his staff sent the man crumpling instantly, his body collapsing with a muted thud.

Zarathyn worked quickly. He dragged the limp form behind the crates, pressing him into the shadows. The man's breathing was shallow but steady. Killing him outright would've been easy —cleaner, even—but Zarathyn saw no honor in ending someone who didn't even have a chance to draw a weapon. For now, he was just another forgotten shadow in this place.

He rose to his full height and surveyed the room. The mana conduits cast flickering light across the space, throwing jagged shadows across every surface. Zarathyn felt the energy around him, a sickening buzz that wormed into his mind. This wasn't the vibrant magic he once wielded in his prime—it was tainted, corrupted by the Dominium's obsession with control. It made his teeth ache and his fingers twitch.

A drone hovered into view, its spherical frame spinning lazily as it scanned the room with a pale green beam. Zarathyn pressed against the wall, his cloak blending seamlessly with the dark steel behind him. The drone's core whirred louder as it approached the crates where he'd stashed the technician's body. It stopped, its sensor light flickering.

Zarathyn didn't hesitate. He raised his staff, a tendril of fire coiling around the tip. With a sharp, whispered incantation, the flame shot forward like a serpent, piercing the drone's core with surgical precision. The machine sputtered once, its whirring fading into a hollow crackle before it dropped to the ground, a scorched husk. Smoke curled up from its shattered remains, the mana core still glowing faintly as if refusing to admit defeat.

Satisfied, Zarathyn stepped over the wreckage, his eyes scanning for the next threat. Ahead, the hallway split into several paths, each marked with glowing signs written in Dominium glyphs. One pointed toward Assembly Chamber Alpha. Another read Mana Core Refinement. The third, Security Hub, caught his eye. A grin tugged at his lips. If he could reach the hub, he could cripple this place from within—disable defenses, reroute drones, maybe even overload the mana conduits and turn this factory into an inferno.

He moved with purpose now, his steps quicker but still careful. The oppressive hum of the machines seemed to grow louder, more frantic, as if the facility itself knew it had been infiltrated. Zarathyn's magic flared faintly around him, heat rippling off his staff. He would burn this place down, one calculated strike at a time.

The corridor stretched before Zarathyn, a

tunnel of cold steel and pale light. The air here felt different, heavier, like it had been charged with static. The hum wasn't the mechanical drone of conveyor belts or mana cores—it was something deeper, something alive. Zarathyn slowed his steps, his instincts prickling.

As he approached the end of the passage, the energy shifted, the hum turning into a low, vibrating thrum. He could feel it on his skin now, pressing against him, testing his resolve. Then he saw it—a shimmering field of energy, its edges warping the air like heat rising off a forge. The barrier pulsed with pale green light, runes etched into the walls on either side, their glow feeding the magic that kept the ward alive.

Zarathyn stopped just short of the barrier, his staff tapping lightly against the floor as he leaned forward to study it. This wasn't some crude piece of machinery; this was Dominium magic-tech at its most insidious. He could sense the layers of enchantments woven into it—wards to repel intruders, traps to incapacitate anyone foolish enough to push through, and a core powered by a mana crystal pulsing with stolen energy. They'd stolen magic and twisted it into this, a lifeless guardian for their lifeless machines.

He clenched his jaw, gripping his staff tightly. For a moment, he considered turning back, finding another way in. But then he dismissed the thought with a snarl. He wasn't here to sneak around their traps forever. He was here to destroy.

"Let's see if they're ready for real magic," he muttered, his voice low and rough.

Zarathyn raised his free hand, calling forth a spark of flame. It hovered above his palm, flickering like a restless spirit. He fed it with his will, shaping it, coaxing it to grow. The flame expanded, shifting from orange to a deep crimson, until it became a roiling orb of fire, its surface crackling with heat so intense it warped the air around it.

The barrier seemed to sense his intent. The runes on the walls flared brighter, the green light intensifying as if to warn him off. He ignored it. This was magic built by men who didn't understand what they were playing with. He'd spent centuries mastering the arcane arts, bending elements to his will, commanding forces that would tear lesser minds apart. They thought their traps could stop him? Fools.

With a sharp motion, Zarathyn thrust the orb of fire toward the barrier. It struck the shimmering field with a sound like a thunderclap, fire meeting magic in a violent clash. The barrier resisted, rippling violently, its green light flaring as it fought to hold its shape. Sparks flew in all directions, burning small pits into the floor and walls.

Zarathyn stepped forward, his staff raised now, its carved runes glowing faintly as he channeled his magic through it. He poured more energy into the orb, forcing it against the barrier, watching as the green light began to buckle. The air filled with the acrid stench of burning mana, the barrier's runes flickering wildly as they struggled to maintain their cohesion.

And then, with a sound like shattering glass, the barrier collapsed. The green light exploded outward in a wave, shards of dissipating magic slicing through the air. Zarathyn stepped through without hesitation, fire still crackling in his palm.

On the other side, the air was colder, but he felt the residual hum of power in the walls. The Dominium hadn't left this place undefended. He could sense it—machines waking, mana conduits flaring to life, and something larger waiting further in, like a predator stirring from its slumber.

He let the fire die in his hand, gripping his staff tightly. The corridor ahead loomed dark and silent, but Zarathyn's sharp eyes caught movement— small, precise shapes skittering along the ceiling, their metallic limbs glinting faintly in the dim light.

A grim smile tugged at his lips. Let them come.

CHAPTER 21

The air split with the sound of shattering magic. The ward screamed against Zarathyn's will, its intricate lattice of stolen spells collapsing in a burst of emerald sparks. Energy clawed at his skin like fire ants, trying to force him back. He didn't flinch. Instead, he gritted his teeth and pushed harder, shoving raw mana into his staff until the barrier gave way with a crack that echoed through the facility like a cannon shot.

The corridor beyond lit up in crimson fury. Alarms screeched from hidden speakers, their sharp wail ricocheting off the metal walls. Overhead, red emergency lights snapped on, flooding the space with pulsing, bloody hues. The rhythmic glare painted everything in stark, jagged shadows, making the already oppressive halls feel like the gullet of some vast, hungry beast.

Zarathyn let out a low chuckle, rolling his shoulders as if shaking off the last remnants of the ward's resistance. So much for slipping in unnoticed. He planted his staff against the floor, the sharp clack swallowed by the growing hum of machinery springing to life. Somewhere deeper inside, gears groaned and mana engines roared as the facility prepared its defenses.

"Well," he muttered to himself, eyes glinting with cruel amusement, "no point whispering now."

He raised his staff, channeling a pulse of fire magic down its length. The runes carved into the wood lit up like embers, sending a faint hiss into the air as the temperature around him spiked. Flames coiled up the staff, licking hungrily at its tip, waiting for his command.

The first wave of drones arrived—a pack of three skittering machines that clattered into view from a side corridor. Their spindly limbs moved with eerie precision, mana crystals glowing faintly at their cores. Crossbows mounted on their shoulders whirred, aiming with mechanical efficiency.

Zarathyn didn't wait. He thrust his staff forward, and the flames at its tip erupted, a roaring jet of fire that turned the corridor into an inferno. The lead drone disintegrated instantly, its mana crystal bursting in a dazzling flash of blue sparks. The others faltered, their metal frames glowing red-hot as the fire engulfed them. One managed a single, desperate shot—a mana-charged bolt that screamed toward Zarathyn's chest.

He sidestepped with practiced ease, the bolt hissing past him and slamming into the wall, where it exploded in a shower of shrapnel. Before the second drone could recover, he swung his staff in a wide arc, sending a whip of fire slicing through the air. It carved clean through the drone's legs, toppling it in a heap of sparking debris.

The third drone tried to retreat, its joints screeching as it scrambled backward, but Zarathyn was already moving. He closed the distance in two strides, slamming the butt of his staff into the machine's glowing core. The crystal cracked, then shattered, sending a surge of mana energy rippling through the drone's body. It convulsed violently before collapsing in a smoldering heap.

The air reeked of burning metal and ozone, but Zarathyn barely noticed. He stepped over the wreckage, his gaze fixed on the corridor ahead. The alarms were louder now, their wail almost deafening, but beneath the noise, he could hear the pounding of boots—human soldiers this time.

Good.

They marched in with practiced precision, boots pounding in unison against the metallic floor, their mana-enhanced armor casting harsh reflections under the relentless crimson strobe of emergency lights. Plates of gleaming steel interlaced with veins of glowing blue mana flickered faintly, humming with an ominous energy. Each step radiated confidence, bolstered by their weaponry—arcane crossbows gripped tightly, their runic etchings pulsing as if alive. The lead soldier raised a gauntleted hand, fingers curled into a commanding fist, and barked an order that echoed like a gunshot in the corridor's narrow confines. Without hesitation, the group snapped into formation, their crossbows leveling toward the lone intruder.

Zarathyn stood unmoving, his staff planted firmly at his side, flames licking at its head in lazy arcs. His expression betrayed neither fear nor urgency, only a calm, almost mocking focus. The fire wrapped around him in flickering tendrils, casting him in shifting shadows that danced like predators preparing to pounce.

The soldiers opened fire. Their volley came with a sharp, snapping hiss as bolts of glowing mana tore through the air, each one a streak of searing light. The assault hit like a storm, deadly and unrelenting. Zarathyn's grip tightened on his staff, and with a deft motion, he spun it in a wide arc. A barrier of molten energy flared to life, roaring with a heat that distorted the air. The bolts struck the shield in quick succession, their impacts rippling across its surface like stones cast into water. Sparks rained down, the corridor filling with acrid smoke as the deflected projectiles slammed into the walls and floor, each one detonating in a fiery burst.

A heartbeat of silence. The soldiers paused, scrambling to reload their crossbows, hands fumbling as they pulled new bolts from quivers lined with runed compartments.

Zarathyn didn't wait. He shifted his stance, planting the staff with a force that reverberated through the floor. The runes carved into its length flared brighter, glowing molten red as he funneled raw magic into its core. A moment later, the corridor exploded into chaos.

A shockwave of fire erupted from the staff, rolling forward in a wave of blistering heat. The flames surged outward like a living wall, devouring everything in their path. The soldiers at the front had no time to react. The inferno slammed into them with brutal force, their armor glowing white-hot as the flames surged through every seam and joint. Screams filled the air, raw and agonized, as the fire melted through flesh and bone alike. Charred remains crumpled where men had stood moments before, their silhouettes blackened into the walls.

The few survivors staggered back, panic breaking their disciplined formation. They tried to scatter, but their movements were clumsy, slowed by fear and the oppressive heat. Zarathyn moved like a predator among them, swift and unrelenting. He surged forward, flames coiling at his heels, and brought his staff down in a crushing blow on the nearest soldier. The impact cracked the man's helm with a sickening crunch, blood and bone splattering as his lifeless body crumpled to the ground.

Another soldier lunged at him, desperation fueling his charge. His mana-charged blade hummed with power, a jagged edge glowing an electric blue. Zarathyn sidestepped with a fluid grace, pivoting on his heel as he spun to meet the attack. His staff lashed out, its smoldering tip catching the man in the throat with pinpoint accuracy. The blade slipped from the soldier's grip as his hands flew to his neck, futilely trying to staunch the torrent of blood that erupted in a violent spray. He collapsed to his knees, choking on his last, gurgling breaths before falling face-first into a pool of his own blood.

The last man standing turned, his nerve breaking entirely. His crossbow hung useless at his side, forgotten in his rush to escape. His boots slipped on the scorched floor as he sprinted down the corridor, his panicked breaths echoing over the fading screams of his comrades.

Zarathyn raised his hand, fire sparking to life in his palm. The flames coalesced into a spear of concentrated heat, its surface rippling as if eager to be unleashed. He didn't hesitate. With a flick of his wrist, the spear shot forward, leaving a shimmering trail in its wake. It struck the fleeing soldier square in the back, the impact driving him to the ground with a force that echoed through the corridor. The body convulsed once, flames bursting outward, before going still.

The corridor was silent again, save for the crackling of lingering flames and the soft drip of molten metal pooling on the floor. Zarathyn lowered his staff, his expression unreadable as he surveyed the carnage. The air reeked of charred flesh and ozone, the acrid stench clinging to every breath.

He exhaled slowly, turning his attention to the next hallway, where the hum of distant engines grew louder. There would be more coming. That much was certain. But for now, the battlefield belonged to him.

Silence fell, broken only by the crackle of flames and the distant whir of more machines waking. Zarathyn wiped a streak of blood off his cheek with the back of his hand, his expression calm, almost detached.

The air around him was thick with smoke and death, but he barely noticed. This was war, and he was far from finished. He turned toward the next corridor, the flickering light of his staff casting jagged shadows on the walls.

The inferno had only just begun.

CHAPTER 22

Zarathyn planted his staff into the scorched floor, the wood groaning under the surge of power coursing through it. His lips moved in a low, guttural chant, the words of an ancient spell spilling into the air like oil over fire. Flames coiled around his body, spiraling upward, growing brighter and hotter until they seemed to sear the very shadows clinging to the walls. The air itself rippled with unbearable heat as the spell reached its crescendo.

The ground trembled, and with a deafening roar, the flame elemental burst forth. It towered over him, a monstrous being of molten energy. Its "skin" was a churning mass of fire and liquid rock, glowing veins of magma crisscrossing its massive form. Eyes like twin suns glared out from a face that shifted between humanoid and beast, its limbs crackling as flames leapt and licked hungrily at the metal fixtures around it.

Zarathyn's gesture was simple—an outstretched arm, a flick of his wrist—but it carried the authority of a battle-hardened mage who commanded forces far beyond mortal comprehension. The elemental, a living storm of fire and molten rock, responded instantly. It surged forward, each step a thunderous crash that made the ground tremble beneath its weight. Its massive form cast a hellish glow across the room, the flickering flames reflecting in every surface like the facility itself had been swallowed by an inferno.

The elemental's molten fist swung downward in a brutal arc, slamming into the conveyor belt with the force of a collapsing mountain. The steel structure groaned, high-pitched and metallic, before surrendering completely. Metal warped and bubbled under the intense heat, its once-solid form reduced to a molten, sluggish pool that dripped onto the floor in glowing rivulets. The machinery shrieked as gears seized and circuits sparked in violent protest, the elemental's fiery assault shorting out the delicate systems in seconds.

A low, guttural howl emanated from the elemental—a sound like the belly of a furnace exhaling. It wasn't content with just breaking the machinery; it sought total annihilation. Massive arms swung again and again, each strike precise yet devastating, each blow sending molten shrapnel flying in every direction. Conveyor belts crumpled like parchment, assembly lines twisted and snapped like dry branches, and towering robotic arms were torn from their bases, their reinforced joints no match for the elemental's raw strength.

Coolant pipes burst under the strain, releasing pressurized jets of water that hissed and evaporated as they struck the inferno. Steam billowed upward in ghostly plumes, but the effort was as futile as trying to douse a wildfire with a trickle. The coolant only served to create an eerie haze that swirled around the elemental, making its glowing form seem even more otherworldly. The beast of flame loomed like a vengeful spirit, tearing through the industrial heart of the facility with single-minded fury.

Electrical fires ignited in rapid succession, crackling along the walls in jagged, unpredictable streaks. Control panels exploded in sharp bursts of light, sending showers of sparks raining down like deadly embers. Wiring melted into blackened sludge, dripping from conduits like tar, while the acrid stench of burning insulation mixed with the heavier, metallic tang of molten steel.

The air grew thick, choking and stifling, as smoke poured into every corner of the room. Visibility shrank to a mere few feet, the chaos turning the facility into a claustrophobic nightmare of glowing embers and shifting shadows. The elemental didn't pause. It ripped through a towering stack of parts, scattering molten debris like a volcano erupting. Each movement was a calculated destruction, a primal fury wielded with precision.

Zarathyn stood unmoving amidst the chaos,

the flames and smoke parting around him as if they feared his presence. He watched the destruction unfold, his expression unreadable, though his glowing eyes flickered with satisfaction. The roar of the inferno drowned out the faint alarms that still managed to sound, their warning cries lost in the cacophony of destruction.

The elemental howled again, louder this time, and hurled a chunk of molten machinery across the room. It struck the far wall with an explosive impact, sending shards of red-hot steel and concrete scattering in all directions. The sound echoed, a booming testament to the devastation that had taken root here.

The facility was no longer a place of cold, calculated efficiency. It was a crucible of chaos, consumed by fire and fury, its purpose obliterated by the wrath of one man and the monstrous force he had summoned.

A squad of robotic sentries rounded the corner, their segmented bodies moving with mechanical precision. Their eyes glowed cold blue as they locked onto Zarathyn, targeting reticles flickering in unison. The first bot raised its weapon, an arm-mounted cannon that hummed ominously.

Before it could fire, Zarathyn thrust his staff forward, conjuring a searing bolt of flame. The fire screamed through the air, hitting the sentry square in the chest. Its metal casing warped and melted on impact, collapsing inward as molten slag spilled from its core. The bot staggered before collapsing into a smoking heap, its glowing eyes flickering out.

The others retaliated, firing streams of energy that lit up the room with sharp, white bursts. Zarathyn spun his staff in a blur, the runes along its length blazing to life. A shimmering barrier of heat flared up around him, distorting the incoming blasts. Energy beams struck the shield, dissipating with sharp hisses and bursts of sparks.

He advanced without hesitation, weaving through the chaos like a flame himself. With a sharp flick of his wrist, another firebolt erupted from his staff, ripping through the head of the next sentry. The impact sent molten fragments scattering like shrapnel, embedding into nearby walls and floors.

The elemental, still rampaging through the facility, snatched up a sentry in one glowing hand. It crushed the machine like paper, the molten heat melting through its armor in seconds. Pieces of the bot dripped from its grasp, hissing as they hit the floor.

The first wave of guards burst into the room, their arrival marked by the rhythmic clatter of boots on the grated floor. Their rifles, glowing faintly with charged mana, were raised with the precision of trained soldiers. The sharp, staccato crack of gunfire followed, echoing like a grim drumbeat against the metal walls. The air filled with the acrid smell of burning mana and gunpowder.

Zarathyn stood his ground, unshaken. The first volley screamed toward him, but with a sharp twist of his staff, he summoned a wall of flame. The bullets disintegrated on impact, leaving trails of vaporized metal and bursts of heat in their wake. The glow of his staff's runes bathed his face in flickering light, the faintest smirk tugging at the corner of his mouth.

Before the guards could regroup, Zarathyn lunged forward, closing the distance between them in a heartbeat. His staff came down with the weight of a thunderclap, the runes along its length blazing to life as it struck the first guard square in the chest. The impact shattered bone and dented armor, a fiery burst exploding outward as the guard was hurled backward like a ragdoll. He slammed into the wall with a metallic thud, his chestplate warped and smoking, the scent of scorched flesh filling the air.

Another guard, quicker than the rest, charged at Zarathyn with a mana-charged blade. The weapon's edge crackled with unstable energy, leaving faint scorch marks on the floor as he swung. Zarathyn ducked effortlessly, his movements honed and deliberate, and sidestepped the wild strike. With a fluid motion, he drove the butt of his staff into the man's stomach. The guard doubled over, gasping as the air was forced from his lungs in a harsh, wheezing grunt.

Zarathyn didn't wait for him to recover. He pivoted on his heel, bringing the flaming head of his staff upward in a brutal arc. The strike caught the guard under the chin, the force snapping his head back with a sickening crunch. A faint wisp of smoke curled from his armor as his lifeless body crumpled to the floor.

The last guard faltered, panic spreading across his face as he began to retreat. His hands trembled as he fired his rifle wildly, the shots going wide and ricocheting harmlessly off the walls. Zarathyn advanced like a predator stalking prey, each step deliberate and unhurried. With a flick of his wrist, he spun his staff, deflecting the stray shots as if they were nothing more than bothersome gnats.

When the guard stumbled backward into a pile of rubble, Zarathyn raised his free hand, fingers curling as a sphere of fire coalesced in his palm. The heat radiating from it distorted the air, the flame pulsing like a heartbeat. He swept his hand forward with almost casual disdain, releasing a lance of flame that streaked through the air like a comet.

The fiery projectile struck the guard square in the chest, punching through his armor in an instant. The impact sent him sprawling, his body convulsing as the flames spread, consuming him with brutal efficiency. His screams, raw and animalistic, were swallowed by the growing roar of the inferno. The firelight danced across the walls, painting the room in hues of orange and red, as the chaos reached its crescendo.

Zarathyn stood amidst the carnage, his staff

glowing faintly as embers drifted lazily through the air around him. The sound of the guard's final, choking gasps faded, leaving only the crackling of flames and the groaning of the collapsing facility. He exhaled slowly, his eyes scanning the room with an icy calm that belied the destruction he'd unleashed. There would be more to come, but for now, the path forward was clear.

The room was a furnace now, the heat so intense that even Zarathyn's wards flickered with strain. He stood amidst the carnage, his staff crackling with residual energy. The elemental loomed behind him, still destroying everything in its path, its fiery form reflected in the pools of molten metal spreading across the floor.

Zarathyn glanced toward the next corridor, his eyes cold and calculating. The facility wasn't finished yet—but neither was he.

CHAPTER 23

The facility teetered on the brink of collapse, every corner of it choked by smoke and fire. Zarathyn moved through the chaos like a conductor commanding an orchestra of destruction, his staff glowing fiercely with runes that pulsed in rhythm with his will. He spotted the massive vat of molten metal suspended above the central production floor, its contents shimmering like a captured sun.

With a sharp motion of his hand, Zarathyn unleashed a lance of fire that struck the chains holding the vat aloft. The links glowed white-hot for an instant before snapping with a metallic shriek. The vat tipped, spilling its glowing contents onto the floor below.

The molten metal hit with a roar, spreading in fiery rivulets that snaked across the grated floor. The guards below barely had time to scream. The molten flood reached them with terrifying speed, consuming boots, armor, and flesh in seconds. One guard scrambled onto a nearby conveyor belt, but the heat warped the machinery, and he tumbled into the glowing pool. His scream ended abruptly as his body dissolved in the inferno, leaving only a charred husk.

Zarathyn didn't linger to watch. His gaze shifted to the tangled network of machinery on the far wall—a labyrinth of gears, conveyor belts, and mana-fueled engines. He thrust his staff forward, channeling a concentrated blast of raw fire into the base of the machinery.

The explosion wasn't immediate. First came the grinding sound of gears failing, followed by the high-pitched whine of overloaded circuits. Sparks showered the room as the machinery seized, shuddering violently. Then, with a deafening roar, the entire assembly detonated in a chain reaction. Pieces of jagged metal and shattered gears shot out like shrapnel, tearing through anything in their path. Entire production lines collapsed in on themselves, crushed under the weight of falling debris.

Zarathyn shielded his face with a flick of his staff, deflecting the smaller fragments as the destruction rippled outward. The explosion's shockwave rattled the walls, and plumes of fire shot up from ruptured mana conduits, adding to the chaos.

Above him, a swarm of drones buzzed to life, their sleek bodies reflecting the crimson light of the flames. They darted toward him in a synchronized attack, their weapons humming with deadly precision. Zarathyn sneered. Raising his staff, he conjured a fire elemental that roared into existence, its form towering and wreathed in molten heat.

The elemental surged forward with terrifying speed, its fiery arms sweeping through the air. The first wave of drones didn't even have a chance to fire; they burst into flames, their metal shells glowing white-hot before exploding midair. The elemental leapt into the swarm, each movement a deadly dance of flame and fury.

One by one, the drones fell, their burning husks raining down like fiery meteors. The floor beneath them erupted into a patchwork of small fires as their remains crashed into the debris-strewn ground. The elemental howled triumphantly, its body flickering as it fed on the destruction around it.

Zarathyn watched, his expression impassive, as the facility continued to crumble around him. The guards who weren't dead were fleeing, their screams barely audible over the roar of the flames. The air was thick with smoke, ash, and the stench of burning oil and flesh.

He stepped forward, his boots crunching on the charred remains of what had once been a thriving production line. The fires danced in his wake, as if bowing to their master, and his staff glowed brighter with every step. The facility was no longer just a battlefield—it was a furnace, and Zarathyn was its heart.

The clang of heavy footsteps echoed through the scorched corridors, a slow, deliberate rhythm that sent vibrations through the warped steel floor. Zarathyn froze mid-step, his senses sharpening. The smoke swirled ahead of him, parting to reveal the squad of mechanized soldiers marching into view. They stood twice the height of an ordinary man, hulking figures of polished steel and whirring gears, their mana cores pulsing like artificial hearts. Each one bristled with mounted mana cannons, the barrels glowing faintly with stored energy. Shields shimmered around them, a faint, crackling distortion that rippled like water in the air.

Zarathyn's grip on his staff tightened, his knuckles pale beneath the ash and blood coating his skin. These weren't mindless drones or hapless guards. These were war machines—built for one purpose, programmed for destruction.

The first machine's cannon hummed louder, its core building power with each second. The glow intensified, a harsh blue light that bathed the corridor in a cold, unnatural hue. Then came the whine—a sharp, mechanical crescendo that cut through the crackle of distant flames—and the weapon discharged. The orb of mana hurtled toward Zarathyn, its edges crackling with energy. It carved through the air like a falling star, leaving a faint trail of distorted light in its wake.

Zarathyn reacted on instinct. His body twisted, moving faster than thought, and he threw himself behind a cluster of steel beams. The impact followed a heartbeat later. The orb smashed into the wall with an ear-splitting detonation, ripping apart steel and concrete in a blinding flash. A shockwave burst outward, slamming into Zarathyn's cover and throwing up a cloud of burning debris.

Heat washed over his face, searing and relentless, and he choked on the stinging, acrid stink of scorched metal. He pressed his back hard against the beams, his fingers tightening around his staff as he fought to steady his breath.

There was no time to recover. A second orb screamed toward him, followed almost immediately by a third. They struck with devastating precision, hammering the beams he'd taken refuge behind. The metal screamed under the assault, groaning as cracks spider-webbed across its surface. Glowing rivulets of molten steel began to drip to the floor, hissing as they met the smoldering wreckage below.

Zarathyn crouched lower, shielding himself as best he could, his robes sticking to his skin from the sweat pouring off him. He felt the vibration beneath his knees—a steady, rhythmic tremor that signaled the machines' advance. They were moving closer, their heavy, metallic strides echoing ominously through the corridor.

His mind raced, piecing together a strategy. The shielded constructs were formidable, their mana barriers shrugging off all but the most focused of assaults. And their cannons? Too powerful for even his finely honed reflexes to evade indefinitely. Head-on engagement wasn't just foolish; it was suicidal.

But shields like theirs came at a cost. Zarathyn knew this, remembered it from years spent studying the intricate dance of energy manipulation. Defensive barriers consumed vast reserves of power to sustain themselves, and even the strongest enchantments had a limit. The trick wasn't in breaking them with brute force—it was in overwhelming them, forcing them to collapse under their own strain.

His fingers brushed the steel floor, slick with ash and molten droplets. The faint thrum of energy from the machines was palpable now, like a low growl vibrating through the air. His mind sharpened, focusing past the chaos around him.

He didn't need to destroy them all at once. He just needed to push them to their breaking point.

Closing his eyes, Zarathyn inhaled deeply, letting the fire within him swell. He felt the ancient power thrumming through his veins, the same force he had once commanded with ease. Now, it was a roaring inferno, demanding precision, control. He raised his staff, channeling the magic through its core. The air around him grew hotter, shimmering with heat waves as sparks flickered and swirled.

With a sharp wordless command, Zarathyn unleashed a firestorm. The corridor erupted in a vortex of flame, a spiraling cyclone that consumed everything in its path. The fire roared with a deafening intensity, its light casting wild, dancing shadows across the walls.

The machines didn't falter. Their shields flared to life, absorbing the inferno as it slammed against them in waves. The air sizzled, and the flames licked hungrily at the barriers, but the shields held firm, glowing brighter with every impact. Zarathyn gritted his teeth, frustration gnawing at the edges of his focus.

He adjusted, narrowing his attack. The firestorm receded, its energy condensing as he poured everything into his staff. The runes along its length glowed molten orange, and the air around him grew heavy, oppressive. The steel beams near him warped and twisted under the sheer heat radiating from his body.

Summoning all his strength, Zarathyn shaped the magic into a spear of pure, concentrated fire. It hovered at the tip of his staff, the flames coiling tightly, crackling with restrained power. He locked his gaze on the lead machine, its shield shimmering defiantly.

With a sharp, fluid motion, Zarathyn hurled the spear. It streaked through the air like a blazing comet, the heat of its passing warping the corridor in its wake. The spear struck the machine's core dead center.

The shield resisted for a heartbeat, flickering wildly, before shattering with a sound like breaking glass. The spear drove deep into the machine's chest, punching through its mana core. For a moment, nothing happened.

Then the explosion tore through the air. The machine detonated in a blinding burst of light and molten shrapnel, the force ripping through its companions. The corridor shook violently as the remaining machines were engulfed in secondary explosions, their shields buckling and failing under the chain reaction.

When the last echo of destruction faded, Zarathyn straightened, his breath coming in short, ragged bursts. The corridor was a scorched ruin, littered with the twisted remains of the mechanized soldiers. Flames licked at the wreckage, casting flickering shadows across the walls.

He lowered his staff, its runes dimming as the magic within him settled. Sweat dripped from his brow, sizzling as it hit the still-hot floor. Zarathyn's gaze lingered on the wreckage for a moment longer before he turned and pressed deeper into the facility, the heat of his conquest trailing in his wake.

Zarathyn's steps were heavy, his body aching with the weight of relentless battle. The thrill of his destruction was starting to wear thin, replaced by the bitter taste of exhaustion. He had torn through the facility like a wildfire, carving a path of carnage, but now, after all that, here he was—staring down the heart of it all. The control room loomed ahead, a glass-walled cage housing the beating core of this mechanized monstrosity: a massive fusion reactor, glowing with an otherworldly light, humming and pulsing with raw power. This was what he'd come for, the source of everything. The way to end it all.

But standing between him and that power was something worse than any machine he'd faced so far. A figure, massive and armored, looming like a tower. The Dominium enforcer was clad in exo-armor, a dark, jagged suit that hissed with the telltale hum of defensive fields. Weapons were mounted on its back—plasma cannons, energy blades, everything designed to rip through flesh and metal alike. Zarathyn felt a cold shift in the air, a pressure building as the enforcer's boots clanged against the floor, advancing toward him with a deliberate, calculated pace.

The thing's helmet gleamed with cruel intent, a reflection of the glowing reactor inside. It growled, a low mechanical rumble that vibrated through the walls. "You've made a mistake coming here, mage," it rasped, the voice distorted and mechanical, like a beast trying to speak.

Zarathyn didn't flinch. The weight of his staff was comforting in his grip, the polished wood slick with sweat, his fingers locked tight around it. The fire within him was a beast that wanted to be unleashed. His eyes flickered with the glow of it, the edges of his vision darkening as the heat threatened to spill over. He knew the enforcer was fast, armed to the teeth, but so was he. The odds had always been stacked against him.

The enforcer stepped forward, leveling a

plasma cannon at him with a sharp whir. The muzzle crackled, charging up with a crackling, deadly energy. The air around it thickened, the humming sound of the weapon's power building. Zarathyn's mind raced. No time for doubt. No time for hesitation. Just the heat of battle, the hum of magic and metal.

He could feel the burn of his magic in the back of his throat, the well of it ready to be unleashed. He tightened his grip on the staff, steadying his breath, every muscle in his body coiled like a drawn bow. The fire flickered in his eyes, alive with a hunger that matched the growing fury within him.

"You should have stayed hidden," Zarathyn muttered under his breath, his voice a rasp of resolve. He wasn't going to run. Not this time.

The enforcer's weapon hummed, the plasma bolt ready to fire. But Zarathyn was already in motion, a blur of action and fury. The air around him seemed to shimmer, the heat from his magic rising as he prepared to strike. The world narrowed, his focus sharp as a knife's edge. The battle wasn't over yet. It had only just begun.

And then, just as the enforcer's cannon flared bright with deadly energy, Zarathyn's magic flared with equal ferocity.

CHAPTER 25

The enforcer's mana cannon lit up the room like a second sun, the energy pulsing so hot it left streaks of afterimages in Zarathyn's vision. He darted to the side as the first shot tore through the air, a thunderclap of sound chasing it. The plasma struck the wall behind him, gouging out a molten crater that dripped and hissed. The smell of scorched steel and ionized air was sharp in his nose, choking and metallic.

Zarathyn rolled behind a terminal, pressing his back to it as another bolt screamed past. The heat of it licked at his face, sweat pouring down his temples and dripping from his chin. He could feel the sheer force of the shots, each one threatening to turn him into ash if he miscalculated for even a moment. The enforcer wasn't just firing wildly; it was herding him, pushing him toward a corner where there'd be nowhere left to run.

The mage gritted his teeth, gripping his staff tighter. He couldn't keep dodging forever. The enforcer's armor gleamed with the light of his fire from earlier, the flames having left no mark, no dent. Whatever material that suit was made of, it wasn't going to burn easily. He had to think faster. Fight smarter.

He exhaled, steadying his mind, and whispered a quick incantation. Flames danced up the length of his staff, hungry and alive. He swung it in a broad arc, and from the ground before him, the fire coalesced into a form—a small elemental, no larger than a wolf, its body made entirely of roiling flame. The creature hissed and snarled, its molten limbs leaving smoldering prints as it bounded forward toward the enforcer.

The enforcer hesitated for a fraction of a second, its visor tilting downward to register the new threat. That was all Zarathyn needed.

The elemental pounced, claws of fire raking against the enforcer's armor. Sparks flew as the creature scratched and battered at the plating, trying to find a weakness. The enforcer swatted it away with a single, brutal swing of its massive arm, the force scattering the elemental into a fiery spray that splattered harmlessly across the floor. But the moment of distraction had already cost it.

Zarathyn surged forward, his staff crackling with heat, flames spiraling down its length. He thrust it toward the enforcer's chest, aiming for the joints in the armor, where the plates overlapped. The tip of the staff struck true, slamming into the armor just beneath the rib plating. A burst of fire erupted from the strike, flaring brightly as it hit. The enforcer staggered back, the force of the blow enough to knock it off balance, though its shields held firm.

The plasma cannon swung around, humming as it charged again, but Zarathyn was already moving. He dove low, skidding across the scorched floor, narrowly avoiding the blast as it carved another smoldering gouge into the ground. Sparks rained down around him, hot and biting against his skin.

The enforcer pivoted, its massive frame surprisingly agile, but Zarathyn didn't give it a chance to fire again. With a sharp motion, he slammed the butt of his staff into the ground. A ripple of fire spread outward, like the surface of a lake disturbed by a stone. The flames licked at the enforcer's feet, surging upward in a blazing torrent. The heat alone would have melted lesser opponents, but the enforcer held its ground, the energy shields flickering as they absorbed the brunt of the inferno.

The shields wouldn't hold forever. Zarathyn knew it. He just had to press harder. "Come on, you oversized furnace," he growled under his breath, circling as he looked for his next opening.

The enforcer let out a guttural, metallic growl, the sound reverberating through the room. It charged, each heavy footstep shaking the ground. Zarathyn braced himself, staff glowing brighter with each passing second, the flames coiling tighter around it like a serpent ready to strike. The fight wasn't over—not yet.

The enforcer lunged, its armored bulk

smashing aside a support column like it was made of paper. The room trembled under the force, bits of rubble raining down, and Zarathyn barely sidestepped in time to avoid the crushing blow. The air roared as the enforcer's fist slammed into the ground where he'd stood, sending cracks spiderwebbing across the floor.

Zarathyn pivoted, using the momentum to swing his staff in a tight arc. The runes along its length glowed white-hot, and a searing crescent of fire lashed out, carving a molten streak across the enforcer's side. Sparks and heat burst from the impact, but the armor held firm. The enforcer barely flinched, turning with mechanical precision, its massive arm sweeping out in a brutal backhand.

The blow caught Zarathyn square in the chest, and the air left his lungs in a sharp grunt. He sailed backward, slamming into the far wall with bone-rattling force. Pain flared in his ribs, sharp and immediate, and a thin line of blood trickled from the corner of his mouth. He coughed once, tasting copper, and rolled to the side just as a massive foot came down where his head had been a moment before. The floor buckled under the stomp, chunks of steel flying like shrapnel.

Scrambling to his feet, Zarathyn spat blood and wiped his mouth with the back of his hand. His grip tightened on his staff, his knuckles white. "Alright, you oversized tin can," he muttered, his voice low and rough. "Let's dance."

The enforcer turned, the crimson glow of its visor fixed on him like a predator locking onto prey. It charged, its cannon discarded in favor of brute force. The room shook with each step, the sound of grinding metal and heavy footfalls filling the air. Zarathyn didn't wait. He darted forward, closing the gap before the enforcer could fully react.

He feinted left, drawing the enforcer's arm in a wide swing, then ducked under the strike, spinning his staff with practiced ease. The fiery tip slammed into the enforcer's knee joint, and this time, the runes flared brighter, a concentrated burst of heat blasting against the vulnerable spot. The joint hissed and buckled slightly, smoke curling from the exposed mechanism. The enforcer stumbled, but its other arm came swinging around, fast and unrelenting.

Zarathyn threw himself backward, the massive fist grazing his chest and tearing through his cloak. The force of the near miss sent him skidding across the ground, but he recovered quickly, rolling to his feet. His heart pounded in his chest, every beat a reminder of how close he was skating to death.

The enforcer didn't relent. It tore through the room, smashing through walls and terminals, turning the space into a battlefield of debris and fire. Zarathyn used the chaos to his advantage, weaving between obstacles, forcing the enforcer to overcommit with each strike. He struck back in quick, precise bursts—a jab to the side, a sweeping blow to the legs, each attack leaving trails of molten steel and flickers of flame in its wake.

But the enforcer was learning. Its movements grew sharper, more focused. It anticipated his next dodge, and when Zarathyn ducked under its arm, it caught him on the backswing. The blow sent him flying, slamming into a console with a bone-crunching impact. The console exploded in a shower of sparks, and Zarathyn crumpled to the ground, his staff clattering beside him.

For a moment, the room was still, save for the enforcer's heavy breathing, the low growl of its servos, and the crackle of distant flames. Zarathyn groaned, pushing himself up on one arm. Blood dripped from his lip, staining the ground beneath him. His vision swam, but he refused to let the darkness take hold.

The enforcer loomed above him, its armored hand reaching down to grab him. Zarathyn's fingers found his staff, and his grip tightened around the heated metal. He drew in a deep breath, ignoring the sharp pain in his ribs, and summoned every ounce of magic he had left.

The runes on his staff burned brighter than ever, blinding in their intensity. Fire coiled around him, wild and untamed, crackling with power. As the enforcer's hand closed in, Zarathyn thrust his staff upward, channeling the fire into a concentrated blast aimed directly at its chest.

The enforcer lumbered forward, the hum of

its overheating plasma cannon sputtering into silence. Its armor hissed, vents releasing bursts of scalding steam into the air as it powered down its ranged weapon. Zarathyn saw the opening and didn't waste a second. His staff shifted under his grip, its runes glowing molten orange as he poured his magic into it. Flames spiraled along its length, coalescing at the tip into a shimmering blade of fire, razor-sharp and pulsing with deadly heat.

The enforcer swung first, its massive arm cutting through the air with a metallic howl. Zarathyn sidestepped, the blow narrowly missing him and slamming into the ground, shattering the steel plating beneath their feet. Sparks flew, and the impact sent a vibration up his legs, but he didn't falter. He darted forward, his fiery blade slashing upward in a swift arc. It kissed the enforcer's arm, searing through the outer layer of its armor. The scent of burning alloy filled the air, sharp and acrid.

The machine retaliated, its other fist swinging low in a brutal attempt to catch him off-guard. Zarathyn ducked, the wind from the strike whipping past his face. He rolled to the side, using the momentum to spring up and slash again, this time aiming for the enforcer's knee joint. The blade bit deep, molten sparks bursting from the wound as gears ground and whined. The enforcer staggered, its balance compromised, but its strength was undiminished.

Another swing came, this one faster and more

desperate. Zarathyn barely had time to parry, his blade meeting the enforcer's arm with a shower of sparks. The force of the blow sent him sliding back, his boots scraping against the scorched floor. His arms ached from the impact, but he held firm, his grip on the staff unyielding.

"Is that all you've got?" he muttered, fire flickering in his eyes.

The enforcer roared—an unnatural, guttural sound amplified by its failing voice modulator. It charged, its bulk tearing through the debris littering the room. Zarathyn held his ground, watching, waiting. At the last second, he sidestepped again, the enforcer's momentum carrying it forward. Its foot caught on a jagged piece of wreckage, and it stumbled, just as he'd planned.

Zarathyn surged forward, his fiery blade a blur. He slashed at the enforcer's exposed side, carving a glowing gash into its armor. The flames licked at the wires and circuits beneath, and the machine shuddered violently, its movements growing erratic. Its plasma cannon began to hiss and glow, the overworked core threatening to rupture.

With a snarl, Zarathyn pressed the advantage. He ducked under a wild swing, his blade carving upward to sever the cables running along the enforcer's arm. Sparks exploded, and the limb spasmed, falling limp at its side. The enforcer roared again, its remaining arm smashing downward in a desperate attempt to crush him.

Zarathyn spun away, narrowly avoiding the blow, and leapt onto its back.

Gripping his staff with both hands, he drove the flaming blade into the enforcer's exposed chest plate, aiming for the glowing core beneath. The metal screamed as the fire cut through, molten slag dripping down in rivulets. The enforcer convulsed, its servos grinding and screeching as it tried to throw him off. But Zarathyn held on, twisting the blade deeper, channeling every ounce of his magic into the strike.

The core detonated with a deafening crack, a burst of light and heat engulfing the room. Zarathyn was thrown clear, tumbling across the floor and coming to a stop against a charred console. He groaned, every muscle in his body screaming in protest, but he forced himself to look up.

The enforcer stood frozen, its armor glowing red-hot, its chest a gaping, molten wound. It swayed once, twice, then collapsed with a thunderous crash. Steam and smoke billowed from its shattered form, and the room fell silent save for the faint crackle of fire.

Zarathyn pushed himself to his feet, his staff still glowing faintly in his hand. He wiped blood from his lip, his breath coming in ragged gasps, and stared down at the ruined machine. "I told you," he said, his voice low and hoarse, "don't underestimate a mage."

He stood over the wreckage of the enforcer, its

twisted metal frame still smoldering. The room was eerily quiet now, save for the faint hiss of molten slag cooling in jagged pools. His gaze shifted to the fusion core on the far side of the control room. The massive structure pulsed with a rhythmic glow, like the heartbeat of the facility itself, the hum of its energy prickling the air. He tightened his grip on his staff, the residual heat from the fiery blade still radiating into his palm.

He moved toward the core, each step deliberate, his boots crunching over shattered glass and debris. The control panels surrounding the core flickered with warning lights, lines of alien script scrolling erratically across cracked screens. Zarathyn tilted his head, studying the energy matrix. It was a delicate weave, a dance of raw power contained by intricate mechanisms. He could feel its heat pressing against his skin, daring him to unravel it.

He didn't hesitate. Planting his staff into the ground, he spread his fingers wide and began to pull. Fire swirled around him, the room darkening as his magic drew the oxygen from the air. His flames licked at the core's surface, probing for weaknesses, until they found the tiny cracks in its shielding. Zarathyn's eyes narrowed, and he poured his will into those fractures, feeding the fire until the core shuddered violently. Sparks erupted from its base, cascading like a shower of jagged stars.

The alarms screamed to life. Red lights bathed

the room, pulsing in time with the core's now-erratic glow. Zarathyn didn't flinch. He twisted his hand, his flames surging into the heart of the machine. The core groaned under the strain, its hum rising to a shriek as its stability unraveled. Panels exploded, spitting shards of metal and glass into the air.

But the collapse was too slow for his liking. He scowled, raising his staff and summoning the image in his mind—a living flame, raw and untethered. It answered his call. A fire elemental erupted from the ground beside him, its form writhing and shifting like molten lava given life. It stood taller than a man, its body blazing with an intensity that made the fusion core seem dim by comparison.

"Clear the way," Zarathyn commanded, his voice low but firm.

The elemental surged forward, its movements fluid and purposeful. It slammed into a crumbling pillar, shattering it into a spray of stone and ash. The ceiling groaned in protest, debris raining down in massive chunks. The elemental swirled its body around him, forming a protective barrier that devoured falling wreckage in a burst of flames.

Zarathyn moved quickly now, his steps steady despite the chaos erupting around him. Flames danced across the walls, consuming everything in their path. The heat was suffocating, and the stench of burning metal clawed at his lungs, but he pressed on. Another console exploded near him, the force of the blast sending shards slicing past his cheek. Blood welled from the cut, but he didn't so much as blink.

The ground beneath him buckled, the core's final death throes shaking the entire facility. The elemental reared up, hurling a wave of fire to incinerate a collapsing beam that threatened to block his escape. Zarathyn's eyes darted toward the exit—a corridor now engulfed in smoke and flame. He whispered a word of command, and the elemental surged ahead, its body slamming through the wall with the force of a battering ram. The flames consumed the barrier, leaving behind a smoldering gap wide enough for him to pass.

The facility roared behind him, the core's energy reaching critical mass. A thunderous crack split the air, and a blinding light erupted in the control room. Zarathyn didn't look back. He sprinted through the smoke-filled corridor, his lungs burning with each breath. The elemental stayed close, its fiery form shielding him from the cascading wreckage.

He burst into the open just as the explosion rippled outward, a wave of fire and shrapnel that swallowed the facility whole. Zarathyn dropped to the ground, his staff braced before him as a shield of flame coiled around his body, deflecting the worst of the blast. The shockwave rolled over him, hot and furious, before finally subsiding.

When the dust settled, Zarathyn pushed

himself to his feet. The facility was gone, reduced to a smoldering crater. He wiped the blood and soot from his face, his breathing heavy but steady. The fire elemental flickered beside him, its form dimming as it waited for his next command.

"Rest," Zarathyn murmured. The elemental bowed its head, then dissipated in a swirl of embers.

He turned away from the ruins, his staff tapping against the scorched earth as he walked. There was no triumph in his expression, only a grim determination. The battle was won, but the war was far from over.

CHAPTER 26

The labor camp sprawled beneath the jagged mountain like a festering scar on the land. A lattice of energy fences wrapped around it, the crackling arcs of blue-white light sending sharp pops into the air with every flicker. The hum of the barriers was low and constant, an oppressive undertone to the desolation that seemed to seep from the very ground. Dust, heavy with the metallic tang of mana, clung to everything—coating the cracked earth, the laborers' sweat-soaked skin, and the air they dragged into their lungs with each labored breath. Every inhalation burned like fire in the throat, leaving a bitter aftertaste that even water couldn't wash away.

The workers shuffled like shadows, their hollowed eyes cast down, bodies bent beneath the weight of baskets piled high with raw mana stones. The stones shimmered faintly, their edges jagged and cruel, slicing into the calloused hands that carried them. Fresh blood seeped into old scabs, smearing the stones with rusty streaks. For every grimace of pain, there was silence. No one dared to cry out. The sound of weakness was dangerous here.

Overseers paced between the lines of laborers like predators stalking wounded prey. Their black uniforms bore the Dominium's insignia, sharp and gleaming on their shoulders. Shock batons dangled from their belts or rested loosely in their hands, spitting occasional sparks like coiled vipers ready to strike. Mirrored visors obscured their faces, reflecting back distorted images of the laborers they tormented. Their steps were deliberate, the crunch of their boots on the brittle, cracked earth a sharp reminder of who held the power.

One overseer stopped abruptly near a boy no older than twelve, his knees trembling under the weight of a basket twice his size. His legs buckled with every halting step, his bare feet scraping against the jagged ground. When the inevitable came—when the basket tilted and spilled its load with a dull, grating crash—the boy froze.

The overseer's head turned sharply, the mirrored visor catching the pale light of the fences. Without hesitation, they unhooked the shock baton from their belt, the weapon igniting with a sharp hiss. "Pick it up," they barked, their voice cold and mechanical, as if filtered through the machinery they so zealously worshiped.

The boy dropped to his knees, his thin arms trembling as he reached for the stones. His fingers fumbled, slipping over the sharp edges, blood smearing across the smooth surfaces. He moved faster, desperation in every shaky grab, but it wasn't fast enough.

The baton struck him hard in the side, discharging a searing jolt of electricity. His body convulsed, his small frame crumpling to the dirt as a strangled cry escaped his lips. Before he could even try to rise, the overseer struck him again, and again, each blow punctuated by the sharp crackle of the baton. The boy's cries grew weaker, his body twitching with every surge of energy.

The other laborers didn't stop. They didn't look. Their gazes remained fixed on the ground in front of them, their movements as mechanical as the overseers themselves. They had learned the lesson the boy was now being taught—the cost of stopping, of staring, of anything that might be mistaken for defiance.

At the far end of the camp, a hulking mech-suit prowled like an armored beast, its every step a calculated display of power. Each motion was accompanied by a hiss of hydraulics and the low whir of machinery, the sound cutting through the camp's oppressive silence like a blade. The suit's joints pulsed with an eerie glow, bands of molten orange and searing blue that radiated an almost unbearable heat. Every laborer within range instinctively gave it a wide berth, shrinking into themselves as its shadow passed.

The pilot sat cocooned within a dome of reinforced glass at the heart of the machine, the thick plating reinforced by veins of mana-infused steel. Their face, partially obscured by the interior's dim lighting, was illuminated in brief flashes by the flickering displays and readouts surrounding them. From their elevated perch, the pilot scanned the camp, their gaze sweeping over the laborers like a vulture picking a carcass clean. Each movement of the mech mirrored their intent, every turn of its massive frame calculated and unnervingly smooth, as if it were alive.

A line of workers shuffled toward the mine entrance, their figures bent and trembling under the weight of mana-laden baskets. Near the end of the procession, a man struggled to keep pace, his leg twisted at an unnatural angle, dragging uselessly behind him. Each step was a battle, the uneven ground conspiring against him as he stumbled forward. His face was a mask of pain, streaked with dirt and sweat, his breathing ragged as he clung to his basket like it was the only thing tethering him to life.

The mech turned toward him with uncanny precision, its joints hissing softly as it pivoted to face its target. Its towering frame cast a long, dark shadow that swallowed the limping man whole. He faltered, frozen in place as the suffocating weight of that shadow settled over him.

"You're slowing production," the pilot's voice boomed from the mech's external speakers, the words distorted and metallic. The tone was flat, devoid of empathy, but layered with a cruel finality that brooked no argument.

The man stiffened, his lips moving in a desperate rush of stammered apologies, though the words were swallowed by the low, menacing hum of the mech's engine. His hands trembled as he clutched the basket tighter, his head bowing lower as if that alone might save him.

The mech's clawed arm moved with startling speed, unfolding like the talon of some predatory bird. It struck with brutal efficiency, the metal claws closing around the man's torso and lifting him clean off the ground. He dangled there, his basket tumbling to the dirt, its contents scattering in a muted cascade.

"Dead weight doesn't belong here," the pilot growled, their voice amplified to fill every corner of the camp.

The claw tightened with a sickening inevitability. The man screamed, his voice raw and piercing as the pressure mounted. His ribs cracked with sharp, audible pops, the sound carrying through the camp like the snapping of dry branches. Blood erupted in violent sprays, spattering the glossy black surface of the mech, streaking its metallic frame with crimson. The man's screams faded into wet, choking gasps before silence claimed him entirely.

When the claw finally loosened, his broken body crumpled to the ground in a lifeless heap, his limbs folding unnaturally beneath him. The mech stood still for a moment, the blood drying in streaks along its polished surface. Then, with a whirring hiss, it turned away, its massive feet crunching over the loose gravel as it resumed its patrol. Behind it, the line of workers moved faster, heads down, their steps hurried as though trying to outrun the memory of what they'd just seen.

The mine loomed like a gaping wound in the earth, its entrance a black, cavernous mouth eager to swallow everything in its path. Jagged rocks framed the threshold, a jagged grin of stone and steel. Inside, the air was thick, heavy with the suffocating sting of mana dust—a fine, silvery powder that hung in the air like a toxic mist. It clung to skin and clothing, settling in the lungs with every shallow, desperate breath. The flickering light from exposed veins of mana cut through the oppressive darkness, casting weak glows of greenish-blue that streaked the walls like a fevered pulse.

The sound of pickaxes clashing against stubborn stone reverberated through the tunnels, each strike a hollow echo in the cavernous expanse. The rhythmic clang of metal on stone was punctuated by the strained breathing of the workers, each exhale labored, each gasp for air a small, futile rebellion against the crushing weight of exhaustion. The sound of grinding joints— creaky and groaning in protest—was an uninvited background symphony. The workers moved mechanically, their bodies bent in unnatural angles from hours of labor, muscles trembling with the strain, but they never stopped.

A woman, pale and thin, stood at the forefront of a vein of resistant mana ore. Sweat poured down her face, staining her ragged clothes as she swung the pickaxe with all the strength left in her weary arms. The impact vibrated up her arms, but the stone didn't yield. She swung again, but her trembling arms faltered, and she froze for a moment, gasping for air as her lungs burned from the effort. Her breath came in short, jagged gasps, the momentary pause betraying the pain gnawing at her body. But the moment didn't last long.

The crunch of boots against the rough stone floor cut through the stagnant air, sharp and deliberate. The overseer's figure loomed in the periphery, his boots clanking with each heavy step. His presence alone stifled the room, as though even the shadows recoiled from him. His face was hidden behind a mirrored visor, a faceless specter of authority.

Without missing a beat, the overseer's hand gripped the mana crossbow slung at his side. His movements were precise, rehearsed, a hunter's instinct honed through years of wielding the weapon.

"Did I say you could rest?" His voice boomed, harsh and mocking, carrying across the cavern with cold amusement. There was no empathy in it, only the satisfaction of wielding control over another's misery.

"I just—" the woman's voice faltered, trembling as she tried to explain.

The overseer didn't wait for her to finish. The crossbow hissed with a sharp, deadly sound as a mana bolt was released, its arc swift and unforgiving. The bolt hit her shoulder with an explosive impact. Her body jerked violently from the force, a sickening crack echoing in the silence. Her scream was cut short as the wound began to smoke, blood soaking through the ragged fabric of her tunic, mixing with the acrid dust on the ground. The burning bolt left a raw, smoking hole in her flesh, and she crumpled to the ground in a heap, her body jerking in spasms as the pain radiated from the wound.

The overseer stepped forward, his boot scraping against the stone as he nudged her fallen pickaxe with the toe of his boot, sending it spinning a few feet across the dusty floor. He looked down at her, dispassionate, as though the life she clung to meant nothing in the grand scheme of things.

"Get up. Or don't. Makes no difference to me. But the quota doesn't change," he said, his voice flat, indifferent to the woman's suffering. The words were more of a threat than a command, an unsaid reminder that the price of disobedience was always paid in blood.

***

The barracks were a pit, a concrete warren where bodies lay in every possible corner, their forms tangled in the stench of sweat and filth.

The air, thick with the damp, clung to the workers like a second skin. The smell of blood and sweat seemed to linger in the darkness, the night offering no respite from the cruelty of the day.

It was late—too late for anything but sleep, but sleep wouldn't come. Not here. Not in a place like this. But there was movement in the shadows, a small flicker of life in the cramped chaos. A young woman, pale and thin, sat hunched over the battered, scarred figure of an older man. His back was arched from pain, the deep, jagged gash across his side testament to the brutality of the work. Blood seeped through the ragged fabric, staining the edges of his tunic, his breath shallow and ragged.

She risked everything to help him, knew the price if the overseers caught wind of her kindness. But she couldn't let him die—not like this, not in this hell. Her hands moved with practiced precision, fingers delicate despite the calluses that lined them from days of labor. She pressed a scrap of cloth against the wound, wincing when the man groaned in his sleep, his fevered brow slick with sweat. The young woman whispered soft words of comfort, though she knew he couldn't hear her. It didn't matter. She wasn't doing this for thanks. She was doing this because it was the only thing left to her that felt human.

She dared not look up, afraid someone might notice her. But there was no one watching. The barracks were suffocating in their silence. The others slept, or pretended to. She had no illusions about what would happen if the overseers discovered her—lashes, perhaps worse. But the risk was worth it. The old man had been kind once, long before his body had begun to break under the constant strain. Now, he was a shell, barely clinging to life. But she wouldn't let him slip away.

Her breath slowed, careful not to make a sound. She finished binding the wound as best as she could with the scraps of fabric she had, feeling a sharp pang of helplessness. Her ration of food had been small, but she'd given part of it to him anyway. It wasn't much, but it was something. He deserved something.

Her fingers trembled as she pulled back, the faintest of gasps escaping her lips as the man shifted. His hand brushed against hers, and for a moment, their gazes met. There was no need for words. The connection was enough. She swallowed hard, fear gnawing at her throat, but there was also something else, something that burned beneath the fear. It was hope.

In the dark, she looked around, ensuring no overseers were lurking in the corners. No one else seemed to be awake, the barracks still as death. But as she sat back, breathing in shallow gulps, there was a noise from across the room. A low, gravelly voice rumbled through the stillness.

"Got a plan, you know."

The woman turned her head sharply, eyes narrowing. The man speaking was older—

grizzled, with the sharp edge of a soldier who had seen too much. His face was weathered, like stone worn smooth by years of exposure. He looked like he'd been carved out of the roughest terrain, his clothes faded and torn from too many days in the mines.

He was sitting up against the wall, his back pressed against the cool stone, a length of broken chain in his hands. It was sharpened at the ends, crude but effective. His fingers ran over the jagged edges with a practiced touch.

"You... have a plan?" The woman's voice was hoarse, as if it hadn't been used in years. She could barely wrap her mind around the idea. Plans? There was no room for plans here. Only survival.

The soldier nodded, his eyes sharp in the dim light. "Ain't much of one yet, but it's something. Gotta be. We can't keep living like this. Ain't no future here, just a graveyard with walls."

The woman hesitated. "The overseers—"

"—Don't care about us." His voice was low but filled with something cold, something sharper than steel. "But there's others. Out there. Waiting. I know it. I've seen it. Ain't no fence can keep us locked in forever."

He glanced at her, a flicker of something in his eyes—a challenge, a dare. "We're gonna learn to fight. I've been teaching the others, showing 'em how to use whatever they can. Stones, chains, scrap metal. Anything that can give 'em a chance."

The woman's stomach twisted. She could hear

the risk in his words, the weight of what he was suggesting. Rebellion. A fight against the Dominium. "And what happens if they catch us?" Her voice was tight.

"They catch us, they kill us." The soldier's expression didn't waver, his voice steely. "But they'll never catch all of us. I'll see to that."

He leaned forward, his voice dropping even lower. "We've got nothing left to lose. No hope here. But there's always a way out. We've just gotta take it."

The words hung in the air between them, thick and heavy with the weight of what they could mean. Hope was a dangerous thing. But sometimes, it was the only thing worth having.

The air in the barracks had grown colder, a chill seeping into the bones of every worker huddled in the darkness. The stale scent of sweat and despair thickened the atmosphere, each breath a reminder of the world that had become their prison. But there was a subtle shift, a quiet rustle in the corner where the old woman sat, hunched but steady. Her hands were rough, gnarled by age and years of toil, but they moved with a tenderness that defied the harshness of the world around her.

She finished helping the man, her actions slow but deliberate, patching up the old wounds that had never quite healed from the constant punishment of the mines. He wasn't much to look at anymore—skin pulled taut over bones, eyes dull

CRAIG ZERF

as if he'd already given up—but in the flicker of light that danced across the damp walls, there was a spark of something left. A flicker of humanity. She gave him one last pat on the shoulder before standing, a sigh escaping her lips as she shuffled toward the far end of the barracks.

It wasn't much, but the boy was there—thin, barely more than a child really—sitting on the cold stone floor, his knees pulled up to his chest. His face was streaked with dirt, his eyes heavy from the weight of too many days spent in this hell, but there was something about him that made her pause. His shoulders trembled, not from the cold but from something deeper, a weight that wasn't his to bear, not yet.

The old woman didn't need to say anything; she could see it in the boy's eyes. The way he clutched his arms tighter around his knees as though trying to make himself smaller, less noticeable. She had seen it in too many faces—fear, hopelessness, the belief that there was no escape, no future, no way out.

But there was always something—there had to be. She reached into her tattered cloak and pulled out a small piece of wood, chipped and worn but still holding form. The carving was crude, uneven, but it had meaning. She had spent her scarce moments of rest shaping it, not because she had the strength for it, but because it mattered. The boy needed something to hold onto. She pressed it into his hands, her touch gentle despite the years of rough labor.

The boy looked at the charm, his fingers tracing the uneven edges, the rough shape of the flame. His brow furrowed, his lips parted as if he didn't understand at first. Then, slowly, something shifted. His eyes flickered—just for a moment—and in that fleeting second, there was a light. Not a brilliant blaze, but a spark, the barest hint of something that had been buried deep within him for too long. The boy gripped the charm tightly, his knuckles whitening. His breath caught, and for a moment, there was silence between them.

The old woman leaned in closer, her voice low, barely a whisper against the thick air. "There's talk. Not just talk, mind you—rumors, whispers from those who've seen it. A fire mage. A man who burns the sky. They say he's striking against the Dominium. He's a spark, kid. A spark that could set the whole world on fire."

The boy didn't move, didn't say a word, but his fingers twitched around the wooden charm, his breath quickening. The flicker in his eyes grew a little brighter, a little more desperate. She could see it. Hope. It was a dangerous thing, hope. But it was also the only thing that kept them going. Without it, they would have all folded in on themselves a long time ago.

He held the charm up to his chest, pressing it there like a shield. The weight of it seemed to settle in his hands, no longer just a trinket, but something more. She didn't wait for him to say anything—she didn't need to. She could see it in the way his shoulders relaxed, just the slightest bit, as if the idea of something—anything—was enough to give him the strength to breathe.

"Keep that close, boy," she said quietly, her voice rough from the years of screaming orders and begging for mercy, but soft now, almost like a prayer. "It might not seem like much. But it's a start."

The boy nodded, slowly, cautiously, as if testing whether it was okay to believe what she had said. And in that brief, fragile moment, the weight of everything around them— the mines, the overseers, the Dominium—seemed to fade, just a little, swallowed by the glimmer of something beyond. Something that wasn't dead yet.

The old woman turned away, but she didn't leave right away. She lingered in the shadows, watching the boy. Watching the way his fingers clenched around the charm. Watching the way he held onto it like it was the only thing that could keep him from slipping into the dark abyss.

And for the first time in years, she felt it, too. The spark.

CHAPTER 27

Zarathyn's boots sank into the damp earth as he moved deeper into the Eternal Forest, the dense canopy above filtering the sunlight into scattered slivers of light that barely touched the mossy ground. The air was thick, weighed down with the smell of rot and the pungent bite of old magic that clung to the very trees. It was a living thing here, the forest—ancient and bitter, with a mind of its own. The trees were gnarled, twisted into shapes that seemed to leer at him, as if the woods themselves held grudges against those who dared step within them.

He knew these woods, every twisted root, every dark shadow between the trunks. The memories of his time as a mage—when the world was still malleable and full of promise—flickered in his mind, but they were ghosts now, far away. He had crossed these lands many times in his past, when he had wielded power as a master of the arcane, shaping the world with a thought. Those days were gone, and in their place was this grim reality, where he could barely muster enough strength to keep moving without feeling the weight of his own exhaustion pressing down on him.

A low growl rumbled from the shadows ahead. Zarathyn paused, the hairs on the back of his neck standing on end. His hand dropped instinctively to the hilt of the sword at his side, the cold steel of its handle familiar in his grasp. The forest was full of dangers—creatures twisted by the System, things that hadn't existed before. Their eyes gleamed like embers in the underbrush, and their teeth were sharp enough to tear through armor.

The growl came again, closer now. Zarathyn's eyes narrowed, and he crouched, slipping into the shadows. He could feel the pull of his magic, a faint hum under his skin. It was a distant thing now, like an old friend who had long since stopped calling, but it was still there. He had to control it, restrain it—no need to draw attention just yet.

The beast was large, the silhouette of its form barely visible through the thick undergrowth. Its breath came in ragged snorts, nostrils flaring as it sniffed the air. Zarathyn waited, his pulse steady, his breath even. A low grunt came from the beast as it moved closer, its paws heavy against the ground. He could hear the soft scrape of claws against rock as it edged toward him. His eyes traced the curve of its massive body, the muscle rippling beneath its fur as it stalked through the forest.

A step. Then another. The beast was close now —too close. He could hear the thud of its paws as it crept up, moving like a shadow through the trees.

The silence broke as Zarathyn sprang from his crouch, his blade flashing in the dim light. With a swift motion, the sword plunged into the beast's side, the impact echoing through the air as the creature let out a strangled howl. Blood spilled from the wound in a thick, pulsing stream, staining the earth beneath them. The beast's eyes widened, its body jerking violently as it tried to lash out. But it was too slow. Zarathyn twisted the blade, his hands steady despite the rush of the kill. The beast let out one final, desperate roar before crumpling to the ground.

Zarathyn stepped back, wiping the blood from his blade with a harsh swipe. The body of the creature twitched once more, the life leaving its eyes as its blood pooled around it. He had killed before, and he would kill again. The world didn't care about the lives lost. It only cared about survival.

The stench of death lingered in the air as Zarathyn took a deep breath, scanning the surroundings. The forest was still, too still. It had always been like this—silent after a kill, as if the land itself waited to see who would be next. He couldn't afford to linger. The Dominium was ahead, its stronghold a looming thing he had to reach. But the forest wasn't done with him yet.

His hand gripped his sword tighter, and he moved on, stepping lightly over the bloodstained earth, his eyes sharp. The path ahead was treacherous, the undergrowth thick and dangerous. There were more creatures in these woods—more things that hadn't seen the light of day in centuries, brought to life by forces beyond his control. But he had dealt with worse. The blood of beasts meant little to him now.

As he pressed on, the air grew heavier, thicker with magic. He could feel the pull of it, like a weight in his chest. The forest was old, older than any of the people who lived on this cursed world. It had witnessed the rise and fall of empires, the endless cycles of life and death. And now, it had become part of the Dominium's grip, twisted and corrupted, a land that had once been free now enslaved by machines and magic.

But Zarathyn wasn't here to play games with the forest. He wasn't here for some pointless skirmish. He was here for something far worse, something that called for blood, for pain, for war. And if he had to carve his way through the forest, he would. Because the Dominium wouldn't stop until everything was broken. And Zarathyn wouldn't stop until he had torn it all down.

The path narrowed ahead, winding between massive trees whose bark was slick and black as oil. He moved without a sound, his boots slipping on the slick surface as he made his way deeper into the heart of the forest. The farther he went, the darker it became. The shadows seemed to grow longer, stretching toward him, as if the trees themselves were reaching out to claim him.

Zarathyn didn't flinch. He had been through worse. He had seen the ends of worlds and the depths of darkness. This was nothing. Just another obstacle to overcome. And if the forest had teeth, he would tear them out one by one.

**

Zarathyn crouched low, his hands pressing into the rough stone of the crag beneath him. The wind bit at his exposed skin, but he hardly noticed. His eyes were fixed on the Dominium stronghold below, an imposing mass of gleaming metal and sharp lines that seemed to slice the very air. The fortress sat nestled in the valley, the land around it cleared and barren, as if the earth itself had given up in surrender to the cold, sterile structures the Dominium had claimed as its own.

The distant hum of power filled the air, faint but ever-present—a reminder of the Dominium's reach, its technology like a sickly pulse beneath the skin of the world. Zarathyn could feel the weight of it in his bones, the unnatural calm it carried with it. It wasn't just a fortress. It was a symbol. A monument to control, to a civilization built on the blood and sweat of those who dared to resist.

From this distance, the facility seemed almost quiet, the occasional shimmer of light catching on the turret's sharp edges or the glint of a guard's exo-armor as they moved in synchronized patrols. Their movements were stiff, mechanical, a far cry from the agility and savagery of the wild things that roamed outside the Dominium's grasp. But Zarathyn knew better than to underestimate them. They were soldiers, drilled and trained, made to kill on command. And they wore armor that could turn even the sharpest blade.

The exo-armor they wore was a marvel of engineering—sleek and heavy with weaponry, almost an extension of the soldiers themselves. Each piece had been designed to give them the edge, to make them untouchable. But Zarathyn was no stranger to untouchable foes. The magic that coursed through his veins still hummed, if faintly, the remnants of power he once commanded with ease. He clenched his fists, remembering the arcane forces he had bent to his will in another lifetime. That power—those memories—weren't gone. They hadn't vanished; they'd simply been buried beneath years of struggle, of survival.

But that wasn't enough. Not now. He had to plan.

His eyes scanned the perimeter, taking in the defenses. The automated turrets were a problem. Their rapid-fire could tear through anything in seconds. But there were gaps, openings in the pattern of their patrols. They weren't perfect. Nothing ever was. Zarathyn's gaze flicked over to the patrolling guards. Four of them moved in unison, their rifles held steady as they swept the ground before them. They weren't paying attention to the sky.

A plan began to form in his mind, simple but deadly. He wasn't going in guns blazing—not yet. But he'd need to make his move when the right moment came. Timing was everything. The slightest misstep, and the whole thing would fall apart.

His hand slid to the hilt of the blade strapped to his side, a solid, worn piece of metal that had tasted more blood than he cared to remember. His fingers brushed against it, the cold steel grounding him. He would need that blade before this was over. The Dominium was no stranger to brutality, and neither was he.

He looked at the walls, at the watchtowers that stood like silent sentinels. They were high, but not unreachable. His gaze drifted to the heavily guarded entrance. Too many eyes, too many guns. He could see the faint shimmer of force fields that encased the main doors, the thick energy shields that hummed with dangerous power. But there were other ways in. There always were.

Zarathyn's lips curled into a tight smile, a flicker of amusement crossing his features. They thought they were safe inside their walls, protected by their weapons and their technology. They were wrong.

Beneath the fortress, the valley stretched out, the craggy cliffs like jagged teeth along the edges of the land. Zarathyn could see the path he would take, winding through the underbrush, hugging the valley floor. It wouldn't be easy, but it never was. He wasn't a fool—he knew there would be blood, more than he cared to spill. But this was bigger than him. Bigger than the ghosts of his past. This was about the future. A future that wouldn't be controlled by the Dominium. Not while he was still breathing.

Zarathyn exhaled slowly, his breath catching for a moment in the cold air. He'd been alone for too long. But that would change. The storm that had been brewing inside him for years was about to break. He had no illusions about what lay ahead. The road would be paved with corpses—some of them his own—but it had to be done. He wasn't here to redeem himself. He was here to end this.

With one last glance at the fortress below, he stood. His movements were slow but purposeful, and as he turned to disappear into the shadows, the weight of the task ahead settled into his chest like a stone. The Dominium had no idea what it was about to face. And Zarathyn wouldn't give them the chance to figure it out.

He crouched low, pressing his palm against the rough stone beneath him. He could feel the earth's pulse beneath his fingertips, the thrum of life in this forsaken land. It was different from the hum of power that filled the air in the Dominium stronghold below. That hum was an unnatural thing, a stark contrast to the raw pulse of nature. But it was a pulse that Zarathyn was getting used to again, however distant it might feel.

He closed his eyes, reaching inward, feeling for

the magic that still lingered in his veins, faint but there. His thoughts twisted, shaping them into a thread of fire. A small spark. It flickered to life in his mind's eye, flickering like a dying ember. A fire elemental, tiny, barely a spark in the grand scheme of things, but it was enough. His fingers twitched, and the ember responded, flaring into a small, crackling flame, its molten eyes gleaming like twin suns. The creature's body writhed and undulated like liquid fire as it skittered out from his palm, forming into something more.

The elemental's eyes locked on him as if waiting for orders. Zarathyn's lips parted just enough for his breath to escape, his voice low but commanding. "Go. I need you to scout the area."

The creature responded with a crackling hiss, slithering into the shadows. Zarathyn's connection to it was immediate, visceral—he could see what it saw, feel its movement as if it were an extension of himself. The fire elemental's vision flickered across the stronghold below, darting between the shadows, its eyes catching every faint shift in the landscape. Zarathyn's mind worked in tandem with the creature, drawing out the patterns, the weak points, the hidden dangers.

Through the elemental's eyes, Zarathyn saw the guard patrols. Four soldiers, each one wrapped in exo-armor that gleamed even in the darkness. The movement of their limbs was stiff, mechanical —too predictable. Their armor reflected light in unnatural angles, casting jagged shadows across the courtyard. They swept the area methodically, heads moving in synchronized sweeps. Every step they took was heavy, clanging like a metal drumbeat.

Zarathyn's gaze sharpened. He watched as the fire elemental slipped closer to the turrets, each one stationed at regular intervals, their muzzle tips catching the faintest glimmer of light from the overhead moon. They were heavy, automated, their designs sleek and angular, designed to tear through flesh with ease. But they weren't invincible. Not with the right planning.

The elemental crawled further, a flicker of heat in the air as it passed by hidden sensors. Zarathyn's sharp eyes caught the subtle hum as one of the sensors blinked to life, sending a pulse through the walls of the stronghold. It was faint, almost imperceptible, but to Zarathyn, it might as well have been a scream. He knew it wasn't the only one. They were everywhere, embedded into the walls, the ceilings—hidden, silent sentinels watching for any disturbance.

With a grunt, Zarathyn dismissed the elemental. It dissolved into the air, its flames disappearing in a brief, sizzling hiss.

He didn't waste time. Without hesitation, he moved, his body flowing like liquid through the rough terrain. The rocky outcroppings of the valley were uneven, jagged, but Zarathyn moved with a grace that came from years of training, his every leap an effortless maneuver. His body was light, but the fire in his veins kept him quick, his jumps boosted with the burst of flame that surged through him. He sailed between the rocks like a shadow, his feet barely brushing the surfaces as he pushed forward, skimming the edges of visibility. Every landing was silent, each jump a controlled burst of speed that carried him to the next point of cover.

He was close now, so close he could almost feel the heat of the facility's walls. His breath came faster, but he kept his pulse steady. He needed to stay calm. His mind churned through the map he had built in his head, finding the weak spots. The service hatch near the southern perimeter. It was small, easily overlooked, but it was the perfect way in.

He darted behind a cluster of boulders, crouching low as another guard patrol passed, their heavy footsteps reverberating through the ground. Zarathyn's eyes locked on their movement, calculating, timing. He was mere inches away from them. A shift in the wind, the scrape of a boot, and they'd be onto him in an instant. But they didn't see him. They couldn't.

He slipped forward again, his path now clearer, the layout of the stronghold etched into his mind with ruthless precision. Every turn, every bend— he knew it now. The hatch would be a challenge, but he could handle it. If he could reach it, there was a chance—a slim one—that he could get inside without raising alarms.

The plan was forming, solidifying in his mind. But Zarathyn wasn't a fool. He knew better than to think everything would go as smoothly as it seemed. There was always a snag, always something waiting to trip him up. And when that happened, he'd have to move fast. But for now, everything was lining up.

He crouched low once more, his body still and silent, as the world around him felt like it was holding its breath. The shadows stretched long beneath the pale moonlight, and the path to the service hatch seemed almost too easy. Too clean. That was the danger of it—nothing was ever simple. Not when the Dominium was involved.

But Zarathyn had come this far. He wouldn't stop now. Not when the price of failure was too high.

CHAPTER 28

Zarathyn crouched low against the jagged stone, his breath slow and steady. He could feel the heat of the facility's energy pulsing in the air, a low hum that made the hairs on his neck stand on end. The Dominium had built its stronghold to be a fortress, and it showed. The turrets, the sensors, the patrolling guards—it was all part of the perfect web they'd spun to catch anyone foolish enough to try and breach their walls.

But Zarathyn wasn't foolish. He was a mage, and he had more tricks up his sleeve than most could even imagine. Subtlety was the name of the game now. The big gestures, the loud explosions—those came later, when the real work needed to be done. For now, he'd use his fire magic the way it was meant to be used: quietly, with precision.

He closed his eyes, letting the pulse of the stronghold fill his senses. His mind sharpened as he wove the magic, subtle as a whisper, threading it into the fabric of the air around him. He focused on the vents, the wires, the metal piping that snaked through the facility. All of it was connected, and he could feel where the pressure points were, the weaknesses in the system. One flicker, one twist of power, and the whole thing would bend to his will.

A snap of energy sparked in the air, a burst of heat that shot through a vent deep within the building. The fire magic rippled out, feeding on the energy in the air, igniting the sensors and setting off a faint alarm. It wasn't enough to trigger a full lockdown, but it was enough to draw attention.

And that was all Zarathyn needed.

He smiled darkly as he watched the ripple of chaos unfold. Guards started moving, their armor clanking as they scrambled in the direction of the false fire alarm. He could feel the shift in the patrols through the web of his magic—one sentry broke away from his post, the others turning their heads in the direction of the commotion. Perfect. The gap was just wide enough for Zarathyn to slip through.

He waited, counting the seconds. His heartbeat drummed in his chest, but he kept his body still, his muscles tense with anticipation. The air around him crackled as he adjusted the flow of his magic, a small flicker of flame dancing on his fingertips. It was a tiny thing, almost invisible in the darkness, but it was enough to catch the eye of the guard closest to the gap.

The sentry's head snapped toward the flicker, and Zarathyn moved. He darted across the shadowed ground, his feet barely making a sound as he dashed toward the opening in the patrol. The sentry didn't even notice. He was already turning, his back to the path Zarathyn needed.

For a moment, it felt like everything was in perfect sync. The heat from the building, the pulse of his magic, the silence of his movements. It was a deadly dance, and Zarathyn was leading.

But then came the wall.

A sheer cliff of stone rose before him, the edge sharp and unforgiving. It blocked his path completely, the top disappearing into the night sky, too high to climb normally, too solid to break through. He could feel the weight of it, a barrier to his progress. But barriers meant little to him. He had ways of making walls bow to his will.

He didn't waste time. His breath quickened as he drew the magic up through his core, channeling the heat in his body into his legs. The fire inside him flared to life, surging like a wave of molten fury. It was no longer the subtle heat he'd used to cause the distractions—it was raw, explosive, and powerful. He crouched, his muscles coiling, and then, with a single thrust of energy, he shot upward, his body propelled by the magic in his veins.

His fingers scraped the rock as he flew, catching the ledge with a sharp, practiced grip. His body hit the edge with a jarring thud, his chest scraping against the stone, but he didn't hesitate. He used the momentum, dragging himself higher, his legs burning with the fire he'd summoned. Each movement was calculated, driven by the magic coursing through him. The heat in his muscles was a reminder of what he used to be—what he still was, deep inside. A mage of power, someone who could bend the world to his will.

He hauled himself over the edge with ease, landing silently on the other side. The ground beneath him was solid, cold stone, but he didn't linger. There was no time to waste.

The magic in him still pulsed, a steady hum that whispered of things long forgotten. Zarathyn breathed out, steadying himself. The wall had been nothing but a momentary challenge, something to overcome. And he had.

But the Dominium stronghold was far from done with him.

Zarathyn moved with silent precision, his every step calculated, every motion deliberate. The facility stretched before him, its cold steel walls looming like a sleeping beast. The air around him hummed with a low, mechanical pulse, a reminder of the technology that had replaced magic in the world. He knew the Dominium was smart—too smart for his liking—and they'd likely prepared traps to catch anyone foolish enough to try and break in.

He wasn't foolish, though.

When he came upon the service hatch, his sharp eyes caught the faint shimmer of the laser grid blocking his path. Thin beams crisscrossed the entrance, deadly as a snake's strike. He'd seen this kind of security before—thin, nearly invisible lines that could slice through flesh and bone with the precision of a master executioner. The grid's hum was a warning, a constant threat waiting to snap.

Zarathyn studied it for a moment, his mind racing through the possibilities. He'd dealt with traps like this before, both magical and mechanical. And he still had the skills—both the old magic and the new tricks he'd learned in this shattered world.

He raised his hand, the faintest flicker of flame gathering at his fingertips. A single wisp of fire danced in the air before him, its tendrils curling with unnatural grace. The tiny flame shimmered with molten gold, a far cry from the roaring infernos of old, but just as deadly. He focused, pulling the fire into a tight ball, letting it flicker and pulse with the energy of a thousand sparks. The fire grew hotter, sharper, though barely a whisper of its power escaped.

With a quiet murmur, he directed the wisp toward the nearest laser emitter. The flames traced a path through the air, twisting and weaving around the deadly beams as it slipped closer to its target. It reached the emitter, then surged forward. There was no explosion, no grand display of fire. Instead, there was a soft crackling sound, a surge of heat that made the air shimmer. The emitter sputtered, then overloaded. Sparks flew like erratic stars, a brief flare of light that vanished almost as quickly as it had appeared.

The laser grid flickered, then powered down with a satisfying hiss.

Zarathyn stood still for a moment, watching the grid go dark. The tension in his muscles eased just a fraction. He could feel the air shift around him, the invisible pressure of the facility's defenses still waiting to strike if he made a misstep. But for now, the path was clear.

He moved toward the hatch, careful not to make a sound, his body blending with the shadows. Kneeling before the mechanism, he stretched his hand out, his fingers hovering just above the cold metal surface. His breath was steady, his focus unwavering. The lock was complicated, a modern marvel of craftsmanship, but it was no match for him.

He concentrated, calling on the fire within him. Not the wild blaze of destruction, but the focused, controlled flame that burned at the heart of every great mage. He poured his energy into the air around him, bending it, shaping it, until a small tongue of flame danced across his fingers. With a practiced motion, he directed it to the locking mechanism. The metal screamed in protest as the concentrated heat touched it, the flames licking the edges with a soft hiss.

It didn't take long. The lock was built to resist, but not to survive a mage's focused fire. The mechanism softened, the metal warping and melting like wax in the heat. The smell of burning metal filled the air, thick and acrid, but Zarathyn didn't flinch. He kept the flame steady, his hand steady, until the lock gave way with a small, almost anticlimactic click.

Zarathyn pulled the hatch open with ease, the sound of metal scraping against metal a quiet echo in the stillness. He didn't rush. Every movement had to be measured, deliberate. The trap had been simple enough, but he wasn't here for simplicity. He was here to make sure the Dominium's reign of terror came to an end.

As the hatch swung open, revealing the dark passage beyond, Zarathyn stepped forward. His heart was steady, his mind clear. The trap had been nothing more than a minor annoyance, but he knew better than to get cocky. The real danger lay ahead.

Zarathyn slipped through the hatch like a shadow, the heavy metal door hissing shut behind him with a sound that made the hairs on the back of his neck stand up. He barely flinched at the noise, every muscle in his body tuned to the quiet. The cold air inside hit him like a slap to the face— sterile, mechanical, lifeless. It wasn't the chill that bothered him, though. No, it was the emptiness. The quiet hum of machines was all that filled the space, a subtle reminder of just how much control the Dominium had over the world now.

The walls, smooth and cold, stretched out before him, gleaming like teeth in a giant's mouth. No windows, no cracks. Just metal and dark corners. Zarathyn's boots barely made a sound on the floor as he moved deeper into the facility, his every step deliberate, silent. His staff was gripped tightly in his hand, the polished wood warm against his palm in contrast to the freezing air. It had been with him for centuries, a weapon that had seen the fall of kingdoms and the rise of empires. Today, it would see the downfall of the Dominium—or so he hoped.

His senses were alive, razor-sharp. He felt the pulse of energy through the facility's systems— thick, oppressive, and alien. It hummed through the walls, sending a chill down his spine. This place was alive in a way he hadn't felt since the old days, but it wasn't magic. No, this was technology, a perversion of what he used to control. Zarathyn's eyes narrowed as he focused on the danger ahead. There was something—someone—nearby, and it wasn't just the machines.

He knew better than to assume the place was unguarded. The Dominium wasn't foolish, even if their over-reliance on their tech made them predictable. There were no alarms, no immediate threats—but something about the quiet made his gut twist. He could feel it, the way the air shifted around him, the subtle disturbance in the energy flow. It was as if the walls themselves were watching him.

He didn't have much time. He could already feel the weight of his past creeping into his mind —memories of battles fought and lost, of magic wielded with reckless abandon, of victories that felt hollow in the end. But he had no choice now. The only way forward was to push through, to reach the heart of this place and destroy it.

Zarathyn's grip tightened around his staff. The familiar weight of it grounded him, reminded him that he still held power, even if it wasn't the kind he had once wielded with such ease. He wasn't the same mage he had been—the one who had torn down cities and bent kingdoms to his will. But he still had his wits. He still had his fire. And that was enough to make him dangerous.

He moved forward, his footsteps barely a whisper, eyes scanning the sterile halls for any sign of movement. His senses tingled with the faintest flicker of magic. It was weak, hidden, almost imperceptible. The Dominium was still using magic, just not the way he was used to. They were adapting, learning, and he could feel their presence like a quiet threat.

A flicker of movement. A shadow. Zarathyn's heart skipped a beat. Instinct, honed by centuries of battle, took over. He moved without thinking, ducking into the nearest alcove and pressing his back against the cold wall. His breath caught in his throat, his pulse quickening as he strained to listen.

Nothing.

Just the hum of machines, the faintest scrape of metal against metal. But he knew. Something was wrong. His fingers tightened on the staff, the air crackling with the faintest trace of fire at his fingertips. He didn't know what was coming, but he could feel it, right beneath the surface. The walls were closing in on him, the quiet suffocating.

The faint whir of the camera was the only warning Zarathyn needed. Mounted high on the corner of the corridor, its glossy lens turned with an almost lazy precision, scanning for intruders. He froze mid-step, his eyes narrowing as it began to swivel toward him. For a single heartbeat, he stayed still, a statue in the sterile hallway. Then, with a sharp flick of his wrist, his staff angled upward.

Fire roared to life at the tip of the staff, contained, controlled—a fiery serpent coiled tight, waiting to strike. Zarathyn muttered an incantation under his breath, the old language rolling off his tongue like gravel, and the flame shot forward. It didn't explode in a chaotic burst; it streaked through the air, straight and focused, a lance of molten heat. The base of the camera caught fire instantly, the plastic and wires melting in a quiet hiss. The lens jerked once, twice, then drooped lifelessly, smoke curling upward like the spirit of a dead machine.

He didn't wait to admire his work. The acrid smell of burnt circuits filled the air, and Zarathyn moved forward, his staff held low but ready. He'd bought himself a few moments, but not much more. The Dominium's tech was faster than most men's reflexes, and it wouldn't take long for their system to notice a missing eye.

Ahead, a faint glow pulsed against the wall—another sensor. Smaller, more subtle, but just as dangerous. Its soft light painted the air in front of it, an invisible net waiting to catch anything warm-blooded that dared step too close. Zarathyn scowled, his lips pressing into a thin line. He knew better than to underestimate the device. One wrong move, one careless flick of heat, and it would trip the alarms.

He gripped his staff tighter and crouched low, his fingers brushing the cold floor as he studied the device. It wasn't just tech. He could feel the faint hum of magic woven into it, a crude layer of enchantment meant to enhance its reach. Sloppy, but effective. It was the Dominium's way—mixing their machines with stolen spells, mangling magic into something mechanical.

"Amateurs," he muttered, the words barely audible.

Drawing a slow breath, Zarathyn extended his hand, his palm hovering just inches from the sensor. He whispered a single word, quiet and deliberate, his voice barely more than a vibration in the air. The magic responded instantly. A small current of heated air curled from his hand, invisible but precise, threading its way toward the device. It wasn't fire—it was subtler than that. A controlled draft of heat, gentle and exact.

The glow on the sensor flickered, dimmed, then flared bright as the heat found its mark. Sparks danced along its edges, and the faint hum faltered. Zarathyn kept his hand steady, his fingers trembling slightly as he coaxed the heat to spread. The device shuddered once, and then it went dark, a faint puff of smoke rising from its casing.

He exhaled, letting the heat dissipate as he straightened. The sensor was dead, its magic shorted out, its circuitry fried. There wasn't a single trace left behind—not a scorch mark, not a crack, nothing to suggest he'd been there.

Zarathyn stepped forward, his pace quick but measured, his staff tapping softly against the metal floor. The hallway stretched ahead of him, quiet and cold, but he knew better than to trust the silence. He'd dismantled two of their defenses, but the Dominium had more. They always had more.

CHAPTER 29

The low, rhythmic rumble of boots striking metal grates reached Zarathyn's ears before the figures emerged. He stilled at the edge of the dim corridor, the faint glow of his staff guttering into near darkness at his command. The sound sharpened, each step deliberate, synchronized— a predator's march. His keen eyes darted to the corner ahead just as they appeared: four guards clad in Dominium armor, polished to a mirror shine that reflected the faint red emergency lights. Mana crossbows hung heavily across their chests, glimmering with a faint blue light that pulsed in time with the hum of the weapons. Their visored helmets betrayed no humanity, just blank, reflective surfaces that seemed more machine than man. The air grew tense, charged with the faint whine of energy barely held in check.

Their movements were calculated, efficient. Not a single wasted motion as they advanced, their heads swiveling slightly to scan the corridor. Then one stopped abruptly. His helmet turned toward Zarathyn like the predatory gaze of a hawk locking onto its prey. The soldier raised his crossbow, and the distorted bark of his voice echoed off the walls.

"Intruder! Halt!"

The command was sharp, clipped, and hollow, the artificial tone only amplifying the sense of menace.

Zarathyn didn't halt. He stepped out from the shadowed alcove with fluid grace, his staff held aloft, the head of it faintly glowing with a pulsing ember of restrained power. His gaze locked onto the squad, his lips pressing into a thin line. For a moment, no one moved. Then the first bolt fired, its blue mana streak leaving a vivid streak in the air.

Zarathyn twisted with practiced precision, the streak of energy hissing past his ribs so close he felt the static crawl along his skin. The bolt slammed into the wall behind him, sending a sharp crack reverberating through the corridor. Another bolt followed almost instantly, then another, the guards' coordination impeccable.

But Zarathyn was faster. His feet barely touched the ground as he flowed into motion, sidestepping the next shot and ducking under the one after that, his movements honed to a lethal, fluid economy. The crossbows' hum intensified as the guards attempted to track him, but he was already inside their rhythm, reading their actions before they could execute them.

Reaching the center of the corridor, Zarathyn slammed the base of his staff into the metal floor with a guttural shout. The ancient words poured from his lips, sharp and venomous, laced with the raw authority of a mage who had once held dominion over entire battlefields. The ground beneath him trembled, the vibrations rattling loose flakes of rust from the walls.

Then came the fire.

It erupted outward in a brutal, roaring wave, licking hungrily at the air as it consumed everything in its path. The corridor was drenched in searing light, the flames casting wild shadows that danced like frenzied specters. The guards broke formation instantly, instinct overriding training as they scattered to escape the inferno's reach. Their armor gleamed brilliantly in the firelight, their movements suddenly frantic against the chaos Zarathyn had unleashed.

The air reeked of burning oil and scorched metal, and Zarathyn's eyes narrowed as he stepped forward, the flames parting obediently around him.

The first guard faltered as the heat engulfed him, his steps awkward and panicked. His crossbow slipped from his grasp, clanging loudly against the metal floor before melting into a twisted, useless heap as the residual flames consumed it. He clawed at his helmet, his gloved hands shaking as smoke seeped through the seams of his armor. Zarathyn moved like a predator closing in for the kill, his steps deliberate, his staff already mid-swing.

The staff carved a brutal arc through the

smoky air, connecting with the side of the guard's helmet. The impact rang out like a hammer on an anvil, and the man crumpled instantly. He hit the ground with a heavy thud, the polished plates of his armor scuffed and dented. Molten droplets from his ruined crossbow hissed as they struck the floor, releasing acrid smoke that coiled around his motionless form.

A second guard surged forward, undeterred by the chaos, his mana crossbow leveled with precise intent. The faint glow of his visor reflected the raging inferno, turning his faceless helmet into a flickering mirror of the destruction. He pulled the trigger, but the shot went wide as Zarathyn pivoted sharply, his staff already whirling in retaliation.

With a sudden snap of motion, Zarathyn spun to face the charging guard, the head of his staff blazing with concentrated fire. He brought it down hard, the tip slamming into the man's chestplate. The impact was violent, sending a burst of flame rippling outward like a fiery shockwave. The guard staggered back, his weapon slipping from his grasp as he clutched at the blackened scorch mark marring his armor. His knees buckled, and he collapsed against the wall, his breaths shallow and strained, his visor fogging with the effort.

The third guard didn't waste a moment. He charged, his steps calculated and swift, a short blade glowing faintly with infused mana clenched tightly in his gloved hand. The weapon hummed with energy, its edge flickering with faint blue light. He swung the blade in a precise arc, aiming for Zarathyn's side, but the mage was already shifting.

Zarathyn leaned back, the blade slicing harmlessly through empty air, its mana-infused edge sizzling as it grazed the lingering heat around him. Before the guard could recover, Zarathyn countered, his staff snapping forward with ruthless efficiency. The blunt end smashed into the man's wrist with a resounding crack, and the blade slipped from his grip, clattering to the ground.

The guard let out a muffled cry, his voice distorted by his helmet, as he stumbled back, cradling his injured wrist. Zarathyn's eyes flicked to the fallen blade, its faint glow already dimming, and then back to the guard, his expression as cold as ice and as unrelenting as the fire that still raged around them.

Zarathyn didn't pause. The flick of his fingers was sharp, deliberate, as if plucking a thread from reality itself. A lance of flame burst forth, narrow and searing, like a blade forged from molten fire. It struck the exposed joint in the guard's armor, the unguarded gap at the elbow. The result was instantaneous—metal hissed and bubbled as the flame chewed through it, exposing raw flesh beneath.

The guard's scream tore through the air, high-pitched and frantic, his arm snapping back instinctively. The smell of burnt leather and flesh filled the corridor, acrid and suffocating. Zarathyn's eyes remained locked on the writhing figure, cold and calculating, as he stepped closer. With a sharp pivot, he brought the butt of his staff crashing down. The strike landed with a brutal finality, the reinforced wood slamming into the back of the man's helmet. A muffled crunch followed, and the guard collapsed, his body folding like a discarded puppet.

The final guard stood frozen at the far end of the hallway. His weapon quivered in his hands, the faint glow of its mana core flickering unsteadily. The guard's helmet tilted slightly, the visor catching the flickering light of the nearby flames. He wasn't just hesitating—he was unraveling.

Zarathyn met the man's gaze—or what little of it he could see behind the visor—with an unwavering stare. The tip of his staff burned brighter, a slow, menacing glow that pulsed with each beat of the mage's heart. The air around Zarathyn shimmered with residual heat, rippling like a mirage.

"I gave you a chance," Zarathyn said, his voice low but heavy with the weight of a thousand battles.

The guard took a step back, his breath audible even through his helmet. But Zarathyn didn't give him time to reconsider. He surged forward, his staff trailing a coil of fire that twisted and writhed like a living serpent. The corridor exploded with light as the fire lashed out, wrapping around the staff as Zarathyn brought it down with precision.

The strike connected with the guard's chest, and the impact was devastating. The metal didn't just dent—it buckled, folding inward like paper under a hammer. Flames roared on contact, searing through the polished armor and finding the vulnerable flesh beneath. The guard's scream was guttural, raw, and short-lived as he collapsed, his body convulsing briefly before going still. Smoke rose in wispy tendrils from the scorched, misshapen remains of his gear.

Zarathyn straightened, his chest heaving with steady, deliberate breaths. The corridor fell silent once more, the echoes of battle fading into the faint, persistent crackle of dying flames. The mage turned his head slightly, wiping a streak of soot from his cheek with the back of his hand. His grip on the staff tightened, the smoldering heat at its tip flickering faintly as he surveyed the carnage.

There would be more ahead. There always were.

The corridor widened abruptly into a chamber dominated by the vault. It was a towering monstrosity of metal and energy, a slab of reinforced steel layered with glowing, pulsing energy shields that hummed like an angry hive. Runes and arcane etchings spiraled across its surface, a crude mix of Dominium engineering and stolen magic, each line screaming a challenge to anyone foolish enough to approach.

Zarathyn slowed, his eyes narrowing as he examined the barrier. His staff tapped against the floor once, twice, as he muttered under his breath, piecing together a plan. The hum of the energy field vibrated in his chest, deep and oppressive, daring him to test it. He leaned closer, tracing a faint rune with his finger. The shield reacted instantly, flaring with bright, jagged light, and sending a sharp crack through the air. He pulled back, his lips curling into something that wasn't quite a smile.

"Clever," he muttered, "but not clever enough."

With a sharp twist of his staff, Zarathyn drew a circle in the air. The motion left a fiery trail, and within seconds, the flames coiled and twisted into form. The air grew hotter, denser, as the flames pulled themselves into a hulking figure. The fire elemental stood taller than any man, its body an inferno of shifting embers and molten rage. Its eyes, twin cores of white-hot flame, burned with an eerie sentience. It let out a low, rumbling growl that reverberated through the chamber.

Zarathyn pointed his staff at the vault. "Break it."

The elemental moved without hesitation. Its flaming limbs slammed against the energy field, and the impact sent a cascade of sparks across the room. The shield resisted, flaring brighter, but the elemental didn't relent. It struck again, harder this time, its molten fists carving streaks of light and fire against the shield. The hum of the field grew erratic, the vibrations becoming uneven. Each strike sent shockwaves through the chamber, the air growing thick with heat and the sharp tang of burnt metal.

The shield wavered, flickering like a dying flame. The elemental raised both of its arms, bringing them down with devastating force. The energy field shattered with a deafening crack, fragments of light scattering like broken glass before dissolving into nothingness. The elemental let out a triumphant roar, its form flickering briefly before Zarathyn dismissed it with a wave of his hand.

The vault stood exposed now, its biometric locks still intact but vulnerable. Zarathyn stepped closer, his staff glowing with renewed intensity. He pressed its tip against the locking mechanism, channeling his magic into a precise, concentrated burst of heat. The steel began to glow red, then white, as the heat intensified. Sweat beaded on his forehead, but he didn't falter.

The metal groaned, warping under the pressure. Sparks flew as the intricate mechanisms inside the lock melted and fused, their precision reduced to useless slag. With a final, ear-splitting screech, the massive door shifted. Gears ground against one another, reluctant and stubborn, but they gave way under Zarathyn's relentless will.

The door opened, a slow, agonizing motion that revealed the vault's interior. Harsh, sterile light spilled out, illuminating shelves lined with gleaming weaponry and strange devices. Blades that glimmered with unnatural sharpness, staves thrumming faintly with stored power, and small, orb-like contraptions pulsing with contained energy. The air inside was cold, untouched, and heavy with the promise of destruction.

Zarathyn stepped into the vault, his staff still glowing faintly as he scanned the shelves. His eyes burned with a mix of determination and something darker—something that remembered power long lost and wasn't ready to let it slip away again.

Zarathyn crossed the threshold into the vault, his boots crunching softly on the metallic floor. The air inside was unnaturally crisp, like the chill of untouched mountain snow, but heavy with an undercurrent of raw energy that made his skin prickle. His gaze swept over the shelves, cataloging the wealth of destruction laid out before him. Mana-laced swords with serrated edges, experimental devices humming faintly with restrained power, and staves etched with symbols he hadn't seen in centuries. All of it stolen knowledge, warped into tools of domination.

His fingers twitched at his side, the itch to seize one of the artifacts almost unbearable. His triumph simmered just below the surface, held in check by the taut thread of instinct. Something felt off. Too quiet. Too... expectant.

He took another step, the staff in his hand crackling faintly as if sharing his unease. And then it came—a voice that froze the air solid.

"Step away from the core, mage."

The words hit like a hammer on iron, deep and mechanical, each syllable grinding with a calculated menace. Zarathyn spun on his heel, his staff already glowing, its flame casting wild shadows against the vault walls. His heart didn't race—it never did—but his grip tightened as his eyes locked onto the figure emerging from the corridor.

The Dominium enforcer filled the space like a storm. It was massive, nearly seven feet tall, its armor a seamless blend of blackened steel and pulsating veins of red energy. Every joint, every plate bristled with hidden weapons, from mana cannons embedded in its forearms to blade edges along its gauntlets. Its helmet bore no face, only a pair of glowing red eyes that burned with an unnatural intelligence. The faint whirring of servos accompanied its every movement, precise and deliberate, like a predator closing in on its prey.

The enforcer raised one hand, the fingers unfolding into a claw-like apparatus that hummed with barely contained energy. "I will not repeat myself," it intoned, its voice colder now, as though the command alone had drained the room of any remaining warmth.

Zarathyn didn't flinch. He planted his staff against the floor, the flames along its length flaring brighter, casting jagged light across his face. "You'll find I'm not much for obedience," he said, his tone sharp enough to cut steel. His eyes flicked to the enforcer's weaponized armor, cataloging weak points in seconds. But the glowing red eyes never wavered, and the energy coursing through its frame screamed of power far beyond what an ordinary guard could wield.

The air between them tensed, alive with the clash of opposing wills. The vault, for all its treasures, suddenly felt smaller, as though it could barely contain the violence about to erupt.

Zarathyn's lips curled into a grim smile, his grip firm on the staff as the flames writhed like living things. He shifted his weight, readying himself. "You should've brought more than that suit," he growled. The enforcer's eyes flared brighter, and the sound of charging mana filled the space, a sharp, rising whine that promised nothing but carnage.

And then the room erupted.

CHAPTER 30

The enforcer stepped forward, each movement smooth as oiled machinery, each step a deliberate promise of violence. The glow in its red eyes pulsed, matching the rising hum of the mana cannons locking onto their target. "You've made a mistake coming here," it growled, the words less a warning and more a death sentence.

Zarathyn didn't bother with a retort. Words wouldn't save him, and he had no patience for bravado. His grip tightened on the staff, the flames crawling along its length like restless serpents. The air thickened, the vault suddenly feeling like the throat of a beast about to swallow them whole.

The enforcer struck with ruthless precision, its twin mana cannons roaring to life. Twin streams of molten light screamed through the air, their passage carving out rippling waves of heat and a sound like the sky splitting in two. Zarathyn flung himself to the side, his movements swift yet measured, the instincts of centuries-old battle keeping him one step ahead. The first bolt obliterated the space he'd been in, leaving behind a jagged, smoking crater that glowed red at the edges. The second passed so close it singed the edge of his cloak, the acrid stench of charred fabric filling his nose as he twisted midair, landing with a jarring thud.

He didn't pause. He couldn't afford to. The enforcer's cannons roared again, this time unleashing a relentless cascade of plasma bolts that chewed through the vault like hungry beasts. Shelves crumpled and shattered under the onslaught, sending shards of glass and fragments of experimental devices exploding in every direction. Mana conduits along the walls hissed and sparked, their protective seals ruptured by stray shots, and the faint hum of the vault's defenses faltered.

Zarathyn moved like a predator caught in a storm, darting and weaving through the chaos with a mix of desperation and calculated grace. Each leap carried him closer to safety, each sidestep narrowly avoiding annihilation. His staff burned bright in his hand, not just a weapon but a lifeline. A quick surge of fire propelled him forward in a streak of crimson light, the heat curling around him like a second skin. He moved faster than human eyes could follow, every step a gamble with death itself.

And then the barrage faltered.

The cannons let out a sharp, mechanical whine as their energy cores flickered, overworked and in need of a recharge. Zarathyn didn't hesitate. His window of opportunity was slim, but slim was all he needed. Planting his feet, he thrust his staff forward, channeling raw power into its tip. A concentrated lance of fire erupted, brighter and hotter than the flames that had carried him through the vault. The streak of molten energy tore through the air like a predator unleashed, slamming into the enforcer's chest with unerring precision.

The flames licked hungrily at the armor, engulfing the enforcer in a blaze that would have reduced lesser foes to ash. For a moment, the room was bathed in fiery light, shadows dancing wildly across every surface. But when the flames ebbed, the enforcer remained, its silhouette unbroken, its stance unchanged. The mana-resistant alloy of its armor glowed faintly, the heat dissipating as though it were nothing more than a mild inconvenience.

The red glow of its eyes brightened, as if mocking him, a silent declaration that his power was nothing in the face of Dominium technology. It shifted its stance, recalibrating, the cannons' hum growing louder once more.

Zarathyn's jaw tightened. The enforcer wasn't just built to kill; it was built to humiliate.

"Of course," Zarathyn muttered under his breath, his tone dripping with frustration. Brute force wasn't going to cut it. The enforcer's armor was a fortress, but every fortress had a crack. He just had to find it before the thing turned him into a smear on the vault floor.

The enforcer lunged, its speed a brutal mockery of its hulking frame. One massive arm swept through the air in a crushing arc, the motion so fast it seemed to blur. Zarathyn ducked low, the wind from the swing ruffling his singed cloak. The force of the missed strike cracked the ground behind him, splinters of stone flying outward. He didn't wait. Twisting his staff in his grip, he lashed out, aiming for the exposed joints where armor met machinery.

The blunt end of his staff connected with the elbow joint, and the impact sang out in a metallic screech. Sparks rained from the point of contact, tiny orange bursts against the enforcer's matte plating. The machine staggered back half a step, its red eyes flaring brighter like it was annoyed by the effort. But it didn't fall. It never fell. Before Zarathyn could follow up, the other arm swung back in a vicious counterattack.

This time, he wasn't fast enough.

The blow struck him square in the chest, and the world spun into a blur of pain and force. His ribs screamed as he was launched backward, weightless for a heartbeat before his body slammed into a towering shelf of equipment. The impact was thunderous, the crash deafening as the shelf buckled under the force and toppled forward. Glass shattered, twisted metal shrieked, and the air was filled with the acrid stench of broken mana cores spilling their volatile contents.

Zarathyn hit the ground hard, the breath torn

from his lungs in a gasping rasp. Debris rained down around him—shards of glass slicing shallow cuts into his arms, fragments of broken metal clattering against his staff. He pushed himself up with a grunt, ignoring the way his ribs burned with every shallow breath. Warm, sticky blood trickled down the side of his face, pooling in the corner of his eye and blurring his vision. He wiped at it with the back of his hand, smearing crimson across his cheek.

The enforcer was already advancing, each heavy step deliberate, like it was savoring his struggle. The twin cannons mounted on its shoulders hummed ominously, their energy cores pulsing as they charged up for another barrage. It was a wall of death and inevitability, and it wasn't stopping.

But neither was Zarathyn.

He forced himself upright, his legs trembling but holding. His breathing was ragged, each inhale a knife to his ribs, but his grip on his staff was steady. The flames along its length flickered and grew, burning hotter, brighter, hungrier. His knuckles whitened as he tightened his hold, his eyes blazing with a fiery determination to match the inferno he wielded.

"Let's try that again," he growled, his voice low and guttural, the words more promise than threat.

The enforcer lunged again, its massive bulk surging forward with murderous intent. Zarathyn didn't retreat. This time, he met the charge head-on, his staff blazing like a star as he swung it in a furious arc.

If brute force wouldn't work, then he'd carve the crack in that armor himself.

Zarathyn's eyes locked on the energy core—a pulsating sphere of raw power that glowed a sickly green, nestled within its containment field. It thrummed in the air like a heartbeat, sending waves of unnatural energy through the vault. He felt the raw power seep into his bones, stirring something ancient and primal within him. But the clock was ticking. If the enforcer regained control of this place, the mission would be a waste of blood and sweat. This was his moment.

The enforcer was recovering fast, its armor shifting back into battle mode, cannons humming as they recharged. Zarathyn didn't have time to think. He had to act now, or it'd all be for nothing. He thrust his staff into the ground, drawing on his magic with a quick, sharp breath. The air around him crackled with heat as he summoned the fire elemental. It burst into existence, a towering inferno of red and orange, its body flickering with flames like a living storm.

The elemental bellowed, its flames licking the vault's walls as it clashed with the enforcer. Heat surged, the air thick with smoke and the crackling of fire meeting steel. The enforcer turned, focusing its cannons on the new threat, but the elemental was faster. It leapt, fists of flame landing on the enforcer's chest, sending waves of heat that distorted the air. The two titans clashed, fire exploding against metal in a cacophony of violence.

Zarathyn didn't waste a second. The moment the enforcer was distracted, he moved. He channeled his magic into his staff, letting it sing through his veins as he focused on the containment field around the core. He could feel the energy pulsing, beating against his senses, like a living thing trying to escape. With a growl of exertion, he twisted his staff, a jagged burst of heat and force erupting from the tip. The containment field buckled, its energy snapping and warping under the strain. Sparks flew in every direction as the field shattered, collapsing in on itself like a dying star.

For a heartbeat, the core was exposed, floating there in all its terrible brilliance. Zarathyn could feel the raw power of it, pulsing through the air like a storm ready to break. He reached out, his hands trembling, not from fear, but from the weight of the energy he was about to contain. The power rippled, vibrating in his palms as he seized it, the heat of it searing his skin but not enough to burn. His mind raced, calculating, adapting. The core was a volatile thing, a weapon in itself, but he had no choice. He had to contain it, or all of this was for nothing.

With a snarl of effort, Zarathyn wrapped the core in a protective barrier of magic. The air around him hummed as the power settled into the containment, its energy crackling like a live wire. The elemental and enforcer continued their battle behind him, but Zarathyn barely registered the chaos. He was focused—his mind locked on the task, the sphere of power in his hands, and the mission at hand.

His heart pounded, the power of the core sending shocks through his bones. But he didn't falter. Not now. Not after everything he had fought for.

The fire elemental faltered, its flames sputtering and flickering as it was battered by the enforcer's relentless strikes. Zarathyn watched it for a split second—just long enough to see the enforcer emerge from the smoke, its armor charred but still standing. That wasn't good enough. Not nearly. The enforcer's red eyes flared, its arms raised, and it took a step forward with the grim purpose of a machine designed for destruction. Zarathyn knew one thing in that moment: he couldn't afford to stay and fight.

The ground beneath his boots shook, the walls groaning in protest. The alarms blared, a mechanical scream that cut through the air, echoing off the stone and steel of the vault. The lights flickered, casting eerie shadows that danced along the walls. The facility was dying, and it wasn't going to give up its secrets without taking everything down with it. That was fine. Zarathyn had made his choice.

He spun on his heel, raising his staff

high. With a quick snap of his wrist, he triggered a chain reaction—a wave of magical energy rippling through the facility's systems, destabilizing its core. The walls shook harder, cracks spiderwebbing across their surface as the lights died in rhythmic bursts. The entire place was coming apart.

Before he could even think, the enforcer lunged, its armored form a blur of motion. Its massive arm swung with the speed of a hammer, aiming to crush Zarathyn where he stood. But Zarathyn was already moving, his staff crackling with heat as he swung it in a wide arc, conjuring a fiery shield that blocked the enforcer's blow. The force of the strike reverberated through him, but he held firm, using the shield to push the enforcer back. With a grunt, he followed up with a swift, controlled thrust of his staff, striking the enforcer in the gap between its armor plating. The blow landed with a sickening crunch, a burst of sparks flaring from the chestplate.

The enforcer's red eyes flickered. For a moment, it looked like it was going to keep fighting, but its body began to seize, its systems failing one by one. It collapsed to its knees with a groan, its joints locking, and then it fell forward with a heavy, metallic thud. The sound of its downfall echoed through the crumbling facility, and Zarathyn didn't waste a second.

he ground continued to tremble beneath his feet as the stronghold began to come apart.

Debris rained down from the ceiling, chunks of rock and metal falling in waves. Zarathyn couldn't waste any more time. He summoned another fire elemental—bigger, angrier, and more destructive than the last. Its form rose from the ground in a flash of flame and heat, a blazing shield that took shape in an instant. The elemental barreled forward, its body an inferno, clearing a path through the chaos of falling rubble.

Zarathyn bolted forward, the elemental trailing behind him, its fiery form protecting him from the worst of the debris. The ground cracked beneath his feet as he sprinted, his eyes fixed on the exit, the walls of the facility crumbling around him. The alarms were still blaring, the facility's collapse imminent, but Zarathyn didn't slow. He didn't need to.

He reached the final hallway, and with a flick of his wrist, he sent the fire elemental ahead, clearing the last of the debris blocking his path. A massive chunk of the ceiling fell just behind him, missing him by inches. His heart pounded, the adrenaline surging as he pushed his body harder, faster. He was almost there.

With one final push, he cleared the last of the wreckage and reached the exit. The entire structure groaned behind him, the sound of a dying beast, and the heat of the flames caught up with him. But Zarathyn didn't look back. He stepped into the open air, the collapsing facility behind him a fiery ruin.

For a moment, he stood still, breathing hard, hands trembling from the exertion. Then, with a final glance at the wreckage, he turned and walked away. The mission was over. But the war was just beginning.

Zarathyn's boots hit the ground with a dull thud, and he didn't waste a single breath before sprinting. His staff crackled with residual energy, but he didn't slow. He couldn't. Behind him, the facility's walls trembled as if they had finally realized their own destruction. The air felt thick, charged with the dying hum of power, and the ground shook beneath him like a beast in its death throes.

He could hear the deep rumble of the explosion building, a low growl that promised nothing but chaos. He pushed forward, his pulse thundering in his ears, until he broke through the final barricade of rubble and stepped into the open air.

Then it hit.

The world behind him erupted in a violent, deafening explosion, a shockwave that tore the air to pieces. Fire and smoke billowed up, a monstrous pillar of flame reaching into the sky, and the earth quaked beneath his feet. The force of the blast threw Zarathyn off balance for a split second, but he dug his boots into the dirt and steadied himself. His heart beat hard, each thump a reminder that he was still alive, still in motion.

He turned just in time to see the stronghold crumble, its mighty walls collapsing inward like the final breath of a dying titan. The explosion ripped through the facility, hurling debris into the air—chunks of stone, twisted metal, and glass shards that glittered in the infernal glow of the flames. The energy core had gone up with the rest, and the sight of it was an ugly reminder of what he had just set into motion.

Zarathyn didn't feel relief. He didn't feel triumph. Not yet. He just stood there, watching the wreckage unfold in front of him, the heat from the explosion licking at his skin. His hand tightened around the energy core, the faint pulse of raw power a constant hum against his palm. It was still alive, still vibrating with potential. But there was no time to marvel at it.

He could feel the weight of the moment settling over him, like the silence before a storm. He'd won this battle, yes, but it was only one in a long, bitter war. The Dominium wasn't the sort to forget an insult like this. They'd come for him, and they'd come hard.

Zarathyn didn't move at first. He let the smoke and ash settle, his eyes scanning the wreckage, taking in the destruction like a man who had seen it all before. The distant echoes of the explosion still rumbled in his bones, but his mind was already working, calculating the next steps. His grip on the core tightened, the edges of his fingers digging into the smooth surface. The pulse in his hand was steady, rhythmic—a countdown to what was coming.

And he knew exactly what was coming.

The Dominium wouldn't let this slide. No, they'd be angry. Furious, even. And that meant they'd send everything they had to finish the job.

Zarathyn's lips curled into a thin, grim line. It wasn't over. It was just beginning.

EPILOGUE

Zarathyn stood at the edge of the ruined landscape, watching as the last embers of the explosion danced in the twilight. The fires from the collapsed stronghold were still smoldering, thick smoke drifting into the sky like a funeral pyre. The task was done, the mission accomplished—if you could call it that.

The energy core still pulsed faintly in his hand, a raw, unstable power he hadn't quite figured out how to harness. It thrummed with potential, but its power was alien to him, something he could feel in his bones but couldn't fully command. Not yet. Maybe he never would. But for now, it would serve. The Dominium didn't care much for subtleties, and they certainly wouldn't hesitate to retaliate for this little sabotage.

But that was a problem for tomorrow. Tonight, the world was his to do with as he pleased.

His eyes swept the horizon. There was still work to be done. Too much work.

He let out a breath, a tired sigh that felt as old as the war he was waging. It had been a long time since he'd felt this—this weariness, this burning desire to do more than survive, more than fight. It was something deeper now, something that pressed on his chest like the weight of the earth itself. Up your game, his mind whispered. You're not enough. Not yet.

He clenched his fist around the energy core, feeling the pulse grow stronger for a moment, as if it too had a hunger, a thirst for more.

He needed to grow. He needed to expand. His magic had been born from fire, from raw destruction. But that wouldn't get him through the coming storm. He could burn things down all day long, but it wasn't enough to rebuild what the Dominium had torn apart. It wasn't enough to give the people something to live for.

Earth magic, he thought, feeling the weight of it as if the very earth underfoot was calling to him. The power of the land. The soil. The stone. It was a magic that wasn't about destroying, but about creating. About holding—about sheltering those who needed it most. People were dying in labor camps, toiling under the boot of the Dominium, broken and lost. They needed a haven. They needed a place to breathe again.

His thoughts turned to the camps he had heard whispers of—places where the Dominium forced their prisoners to work until they broke, until they were nothing more than husks of their former selves. The people there didn't even know what hope felt like anymore. But Zarathyn? He knew hope. He knew it like a secret buried deep in his heart.

And that secret was this: He could make it better.

The land had answers. The core was just one piece, and it was a weapon—a powerful one—but it wasn't a solution. The solution was the earth beneath his feet. It was time to dig in, not just with his magic, but with every last ounce of will he had left.

He had to create something. A place where the people in the labor camps could rise from the ashes. A place that would stand as a defiance against everything the Dominium stood for. A sanctuary that would not only shelter them physically, but give them something the Dominium couldn't touch: hope. The kind of hope that made people rise up, made them fight.

He turned away from the wreckage of the stronghold, eyes hardening as his fingers clenched around the energy core. It was time.

The Dominium was big, but it was bloated. Weak. And when their walls began to crumble—whether by his hand or the hands of those who believed in his vision—they would understand something that had eluded them for far too long.

Zarathyn could almost hear it in his head, a chorus of voices crying out for freedom. For justice. For the chance to live again.

The earth would bend to his will. The labor camps would be freed. And in time, the people would rise.

He closed his eyes for a moment, feeling the pulse of magic in his veins, the hum of possibility. A deep breath, and then he opened his eyes again.

It starts now.

Author's Note

Thank you. Truly, from the bottom of my heart, thank you for joining me on this journey. Writing this book has been a wild ride, full of late nights, far too much caffeine, and moments where I wasn't sure the words would ever make it to the page. But knowing you're out there, turning these pages, made every second worth it.

Zarathyn's story is just beginning, and I hope you've enjoyed watching him fight, struggle, and grow as much as I've enjoyed crafting his world. There's so much more to come—bigger battles, deeper mysteries, and challenges that will test him in ways even he can't imagine. And I'm thrilled to have you along for the ride.

If you enjoyed the book, please consider leaving a review or sharing it with a friend. Your support is what makes all of this possible. It helps keep the story alive and fuels the next installment.

Once again, thank you for being here, for taking a chance on this story, and for believing in heroes who refuse to quit, even when the odds are stacked against them.

Until next time,

Craig

Made in United States
North Haven, CT
06 June 2025

69579289R00162